Disney · PIXAR

TOY STORY 4

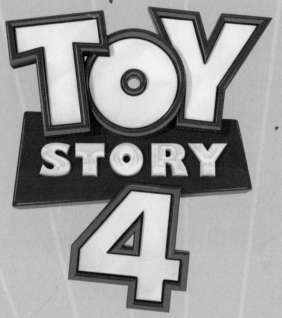

DISNEY · PIXAR

TOY STORY 4

DARK HORSE BOOKS

DARK HORSE BOOKS

PRESIDENT AND PUBLISHER Mike Richardson
EDITORS Shantel LaRocque and Freddye Miller
ASSISTANT EDITORS Brett Israel and Judy Khuu
DESIGNER Sarah Terry
DIGITAL ART TECHNICIAN Christianne Gillenardo-Goudreau

Neil Hankerson (Executive Vice President), Tom Weddle (Chief Financial Officer), Randy Stradley (Vice President of Publishing), Nick McWhorter (Chief Business Development Officer), Dale LaFountain (Chief Information Officer), Matt Parkinson (Vice President of Marketing), Cara Niece (Vice President of Production and Scheduling), Mark Bernardi (Vice President of Book Trade and Digital Sales), Ken Lizzi (General Counsel), Dave Marshall (Editor in Chief), Davey Estrada (Editorial Director), Chris Warner (Senior Books Editor), Cary Grazzini (Director of Specialty Projects), Lia Ribacchi (Art Director), Vanessa Todd-Holmes (Director of Print Purchasing), Matt Dryer (Director of Digital Art and Prepress), Michael Gombos (Senior Director of Licensed Publications), Kari Yadro (Director of Custom Programs), Kari Torson (Director of International Licensing) Sean Brice (Director of Trade Sales)

DISNEY PUBLISHING WORLDWIDE GLOBAL MAGAZINES, COMICS AND PARTWORKS
PUBLISHER Lynn Waggoner · **EDITORIAL TEAM** Bianca Coletti (Director, Magazines), Guido Frazzini (Director, Comics), Carlotta Quattrocolo (Executive Editor), Stefano Ambrosio (Executive Editor, New IP), Camilla Vedove (Senior Manager, Editorial Development), Behnoosh Khalili (Senior Editor), Julie Dorris (Senior Editor), Mina Riazi (Assistant Editor), Jonathan Manning (Assistant Editor) · **DESIGN** Enrico Soave (Senior Designer) · **ART** Ken Shue (VP, Global Art), Manny Mederos (Senior Illustration Manager, Comics and Magazines), Roberto Santillo (Creative Director), Marco Ghiglione (Creative Manager), Stefano Attardi (Computer Art Designer) · **PORTFOLIO MANAGEMENT** Olivia Ciancarelli (Director) · **BUSINESS & MARKETING** Mariantonietta Galla (Marketing Manager), Virpi Korhonen (Editorial Manager)

Published by Dark Horse Books
A division of Dark Horse Comics LLC
10956 SE Main Street, Milwaukie, OR 97222

DarkHorse.com
To find a comics shop in your area, visit comicshoplocator.com

First edition: June 2019 | ISBN 978-1-50671-265-9
Digital ISBN 978-1-50671-282-6
1 3 5 7 9 10 8 6 4 2
Printed in the United States of America

SCRIPT BY
Haden Blackman

COLOR ART BY
Tomato Farm Color Team

LETTERS BY
Jimmy Betancourt of Comicraft

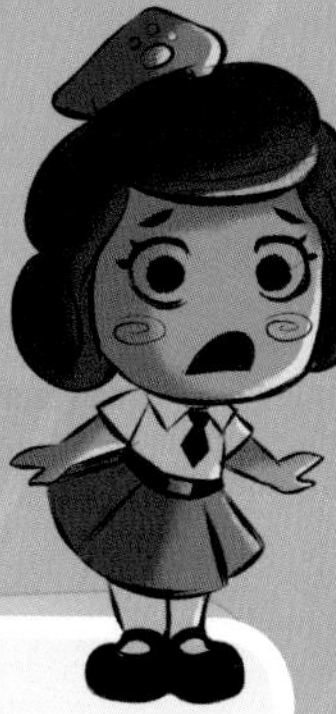

LOST AND FOUND
Art by Ivan Shavrin

DUKE CABOOM'S STUNT SPECTACULAR
Art by Tommaso Renieri

CHIP OFF THE BLOCK
Art by Rosa La Barbera

AFTERNOON AT THE STAR ADVENTURER
Art by Veronica Di Lorenzo

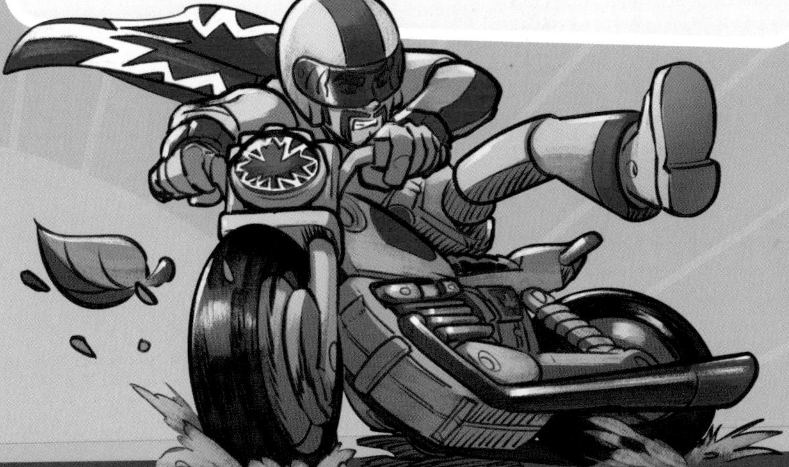

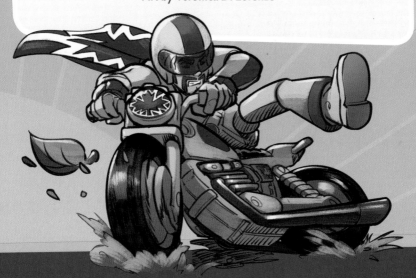

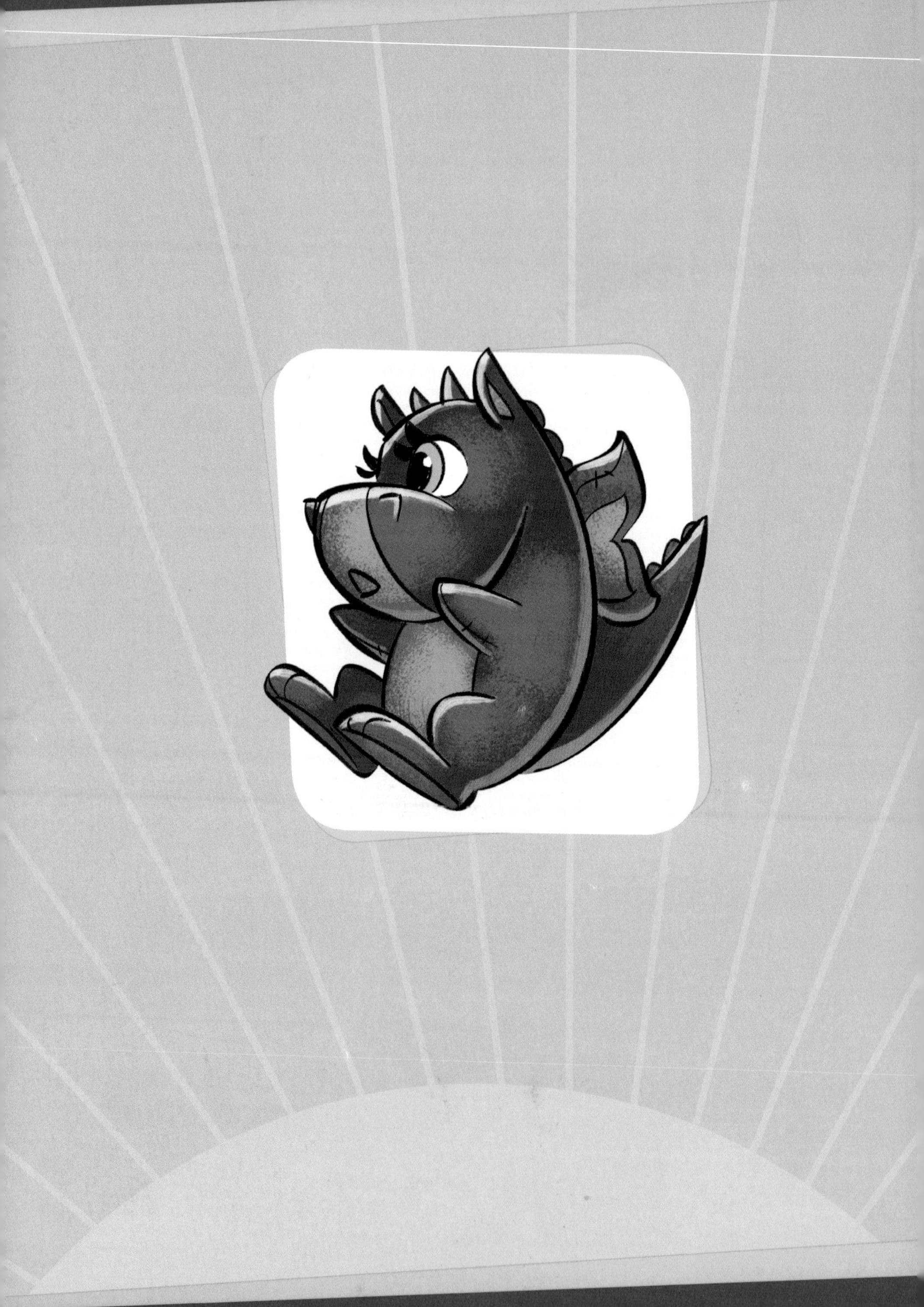

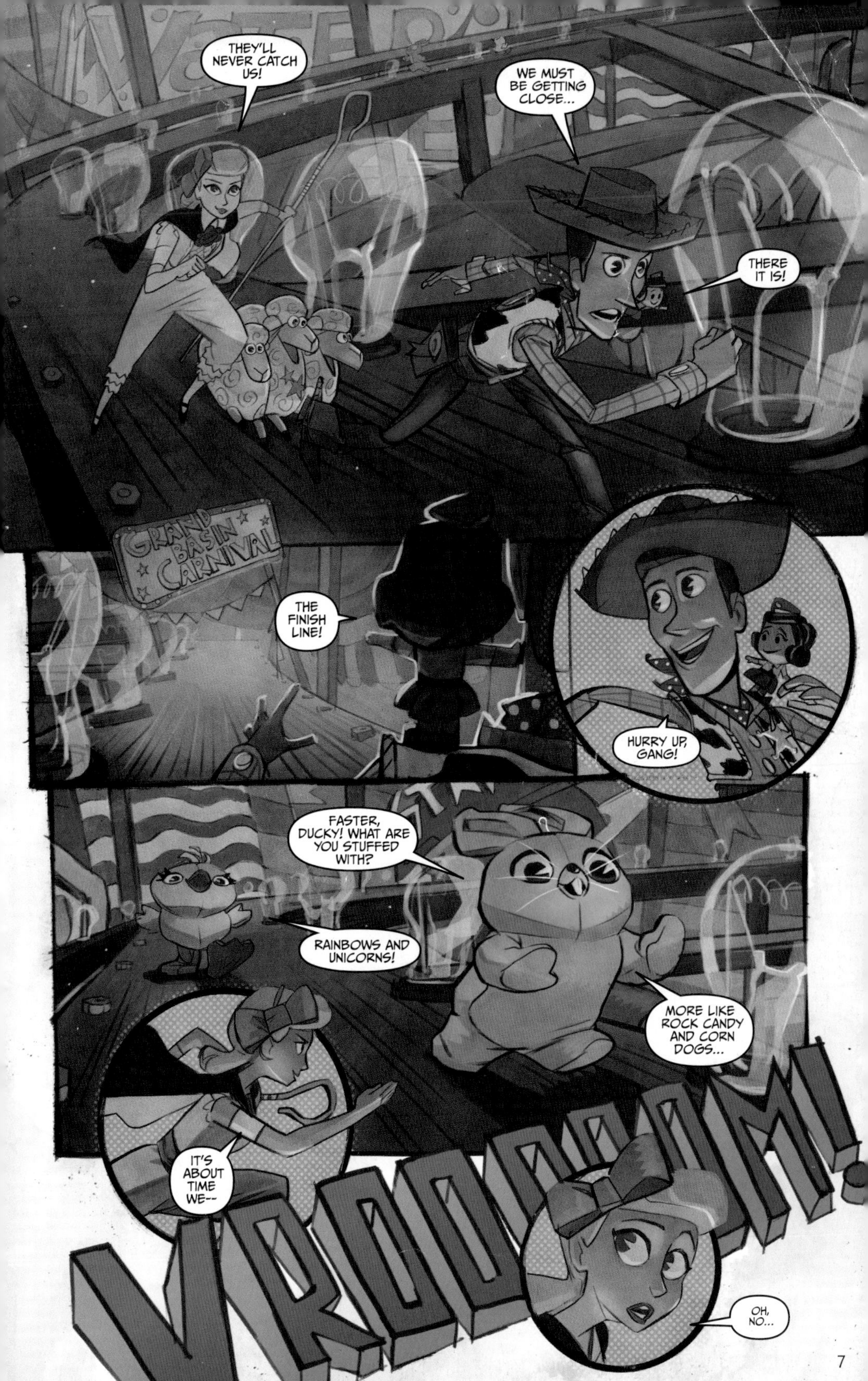
THEY'LL NEVER CATCH US!
WE MUST BE GETTING CLOSE...
THERE IT IS!
GRAND BASIN CARNIVAL
THE FINISH LINE!
HURRY UP, GANG!
FASTER, DUCKY! WHAT ARE YOU STUFFED WITH?
RAINBOWS AND UNICORNS!
MORE LIKE ROCK CANDY AND CORN DOGS...
IT'S ABOUT TIME WE--
VROOOOOOM!
OH, NO...

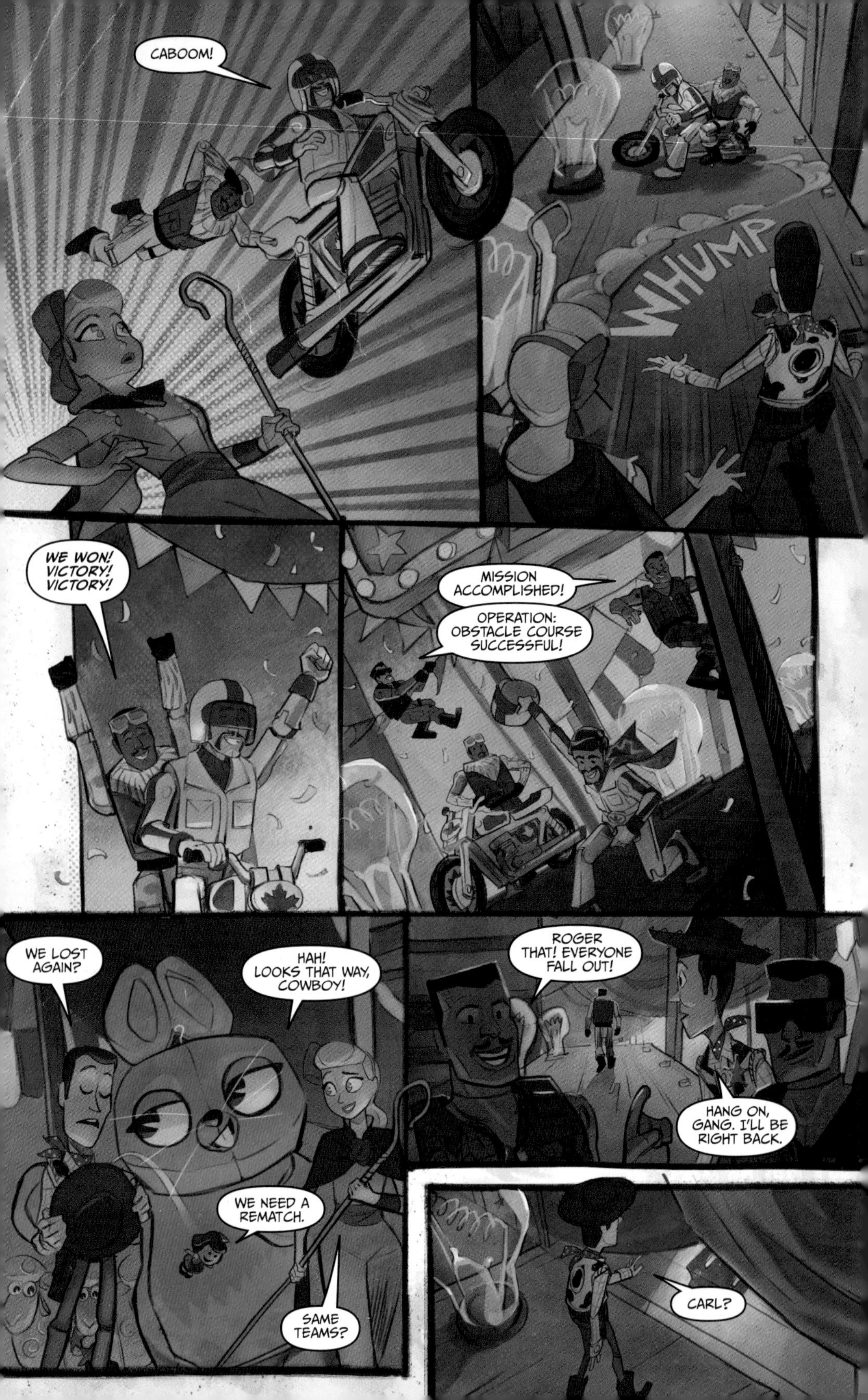
CABOOM!
WHUMP
WE WON! VICTORY! VICTORY!
MISSION ACCOMPLISHED!
OPERATION: OBSTACLE COURSE SUCCESSFUL!
WE LOST AGAIN?
HAH! LOOKS THAT WAY, COWBOY!
WE NEED A REMATCH.
SAME TEAMS?
ROGER THAT! EVERYONE FALL OUT!
HANG ON, GANG. I'LL BE RIGHT BACK.
CARL?

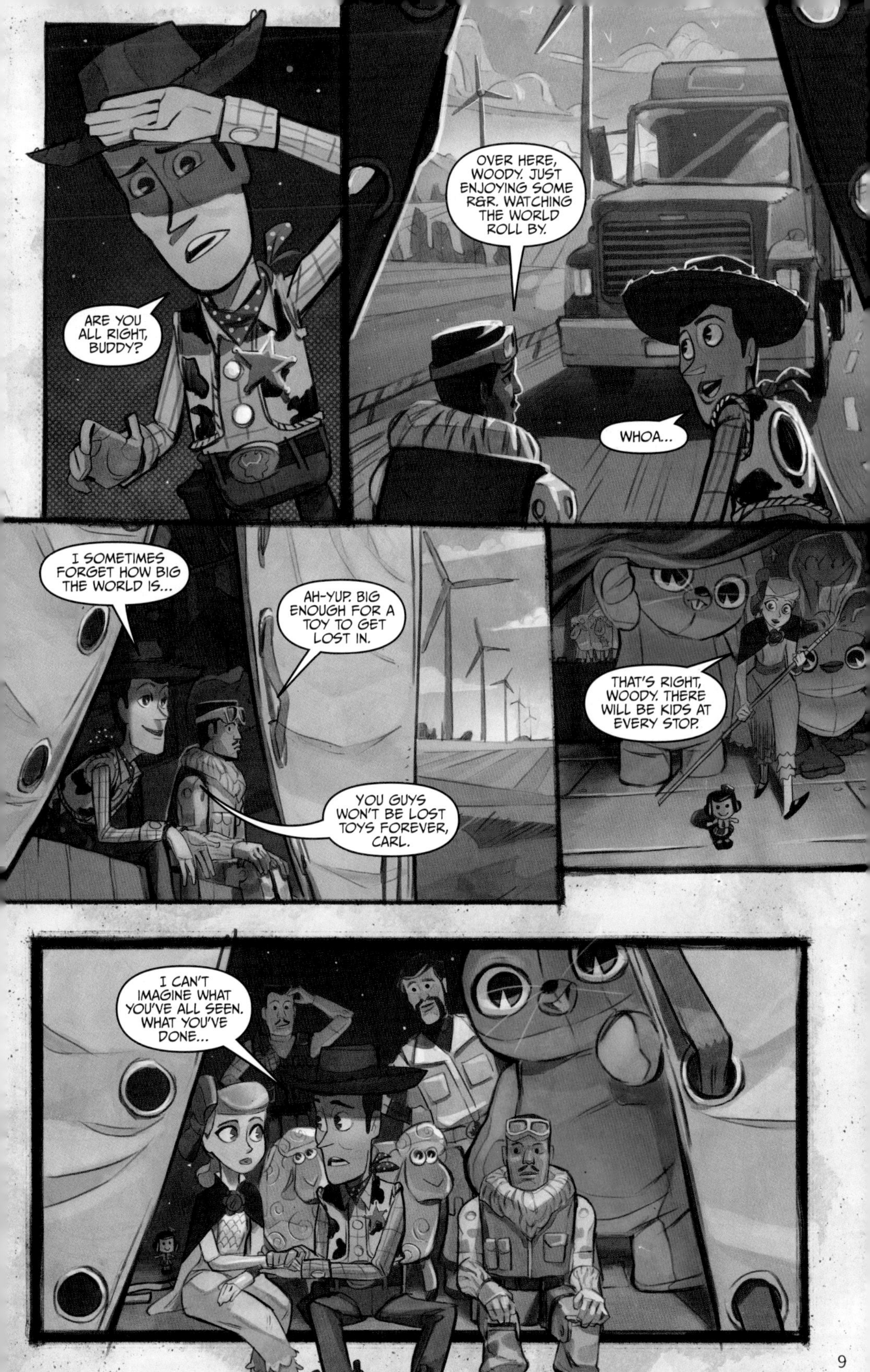
ARE YOU ALL RIGHT, BUDDY?
OVER HERE, WOODY. JUST ENJOYING SOME R&R. WATCHING THE WORLD ROLL BY.
WHOA...
I SOMETIMES FORGET HOW BIG THE WORLD IS...
AH-YUP. BIG ENOUGH FOR A TOY TO GET LOST IN.
YOU GUYS WON'T BE LOST TOYS FOREVER, CARL.
THAT'S RIGHT, WOODY. THERE WILL BE KIDS AT EVERY STOP.
I CAN'T IMAGINE WHAT YOU'VE ALL SEEN. WHAT YOU'VE DONE...

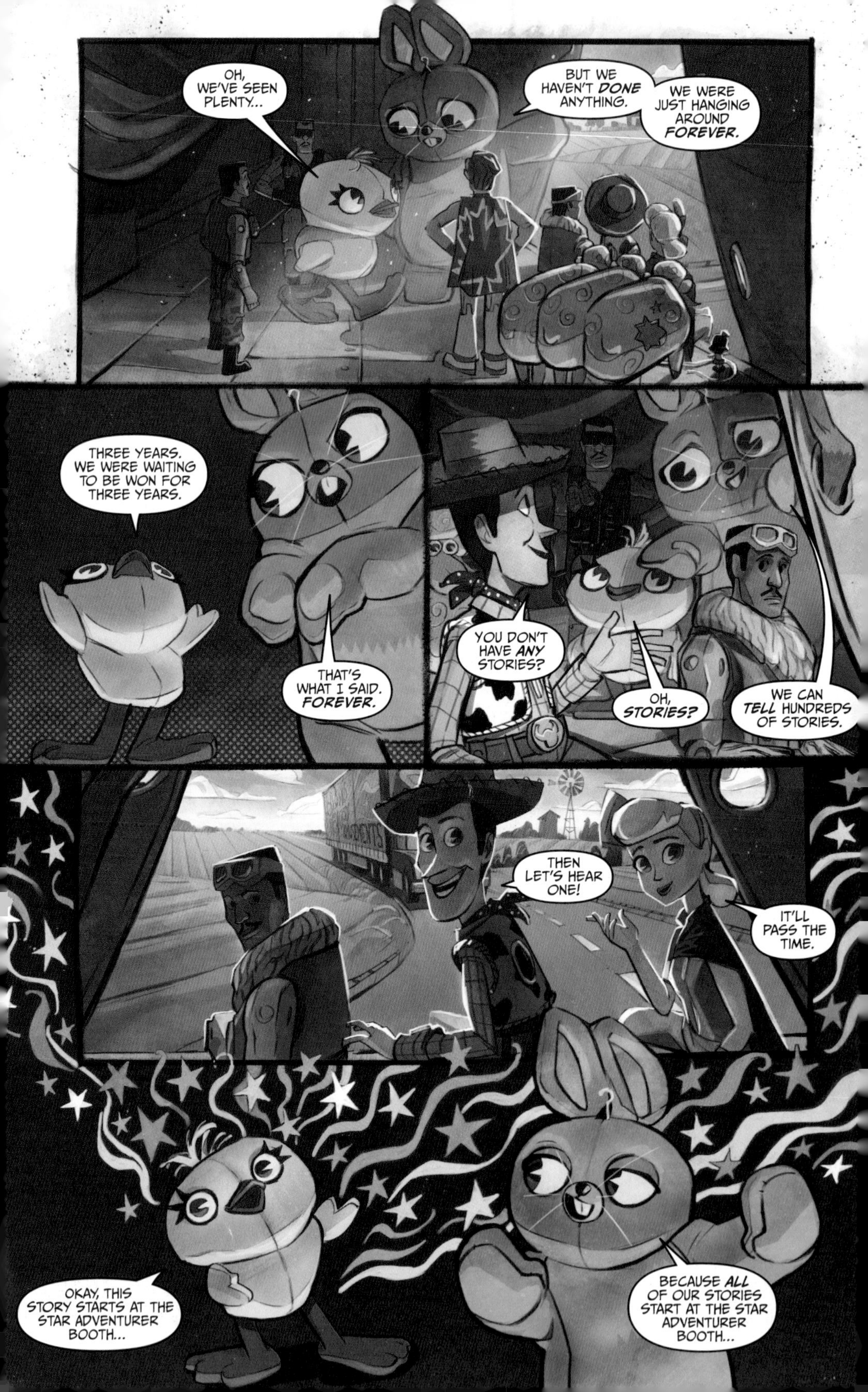
OH, WE'VE SEEN PLENTY...
BUT WE HAVEN'T DONE ANYTHING.
WE WERE JUST HANGING AROUND FOREVER.
THREE YEARS. WE WERE WAITING TO BE WON FOR THREE YEARS.
THAT'S WHAT I SAID. FOREVER.
YOU DON'T HAVE ANY STORIES?
OH, STORIES?
WE CAN TELL HUNDREDS OF STORIES.
THEN LET'S HEAR ONE!
IT'LL PASS THE TIME.
OKAY, THIS STORY STARTS AT THE STAR ADVENTURER BOOTH...
BECAUSE ALL OF OUR STORIES START AT THE STAR ADVENTURER BOOTH...

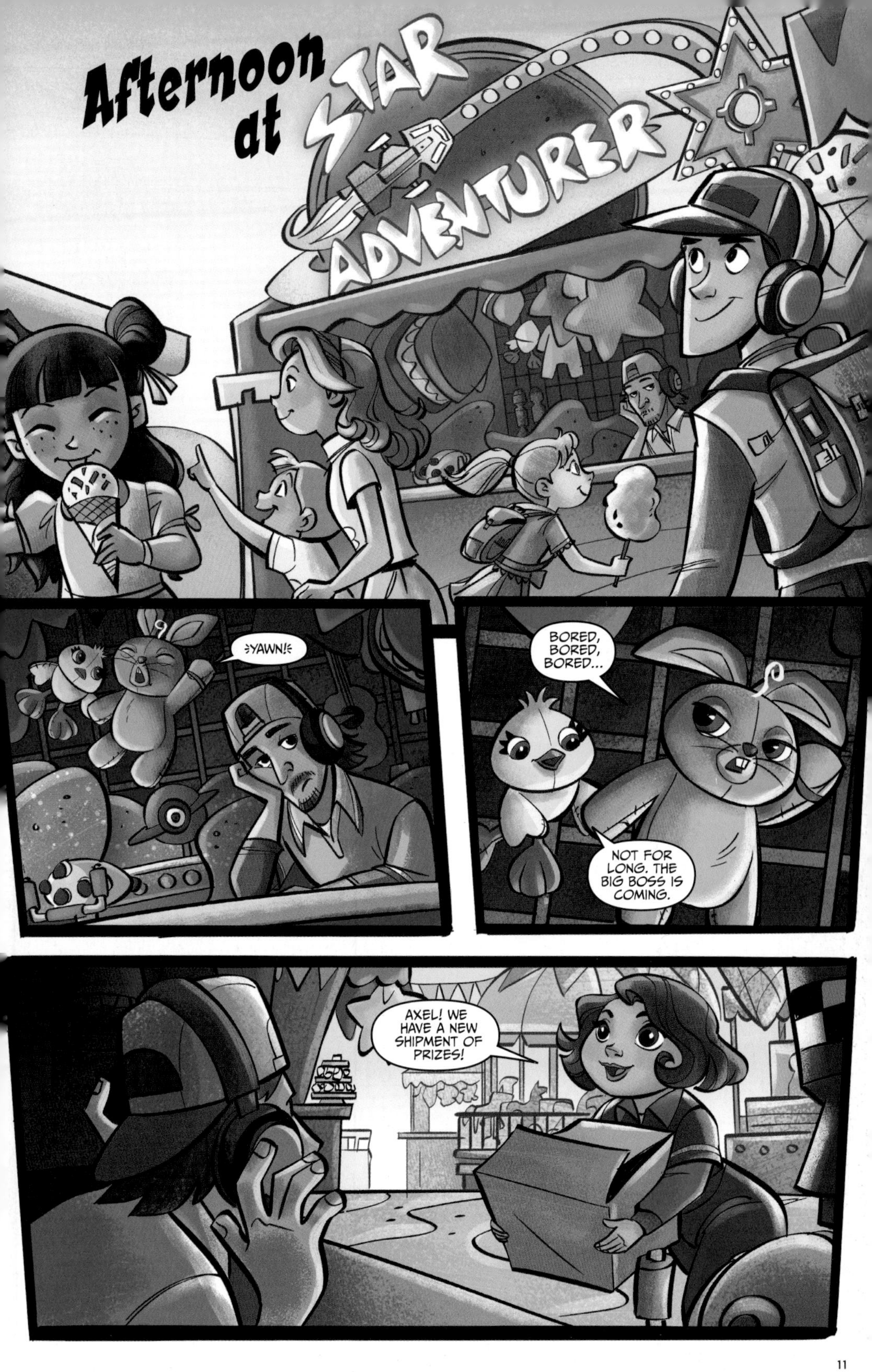

Afternoon at
STAR ADVENTURER
ƎYAWN!Ǝ
BORED, BORED, BORED...
NOT FOR LONG. THE BIG BOSS IS COMING.
AXEL! WE HAVE A NEW SHIPMENT OF PRIZES!

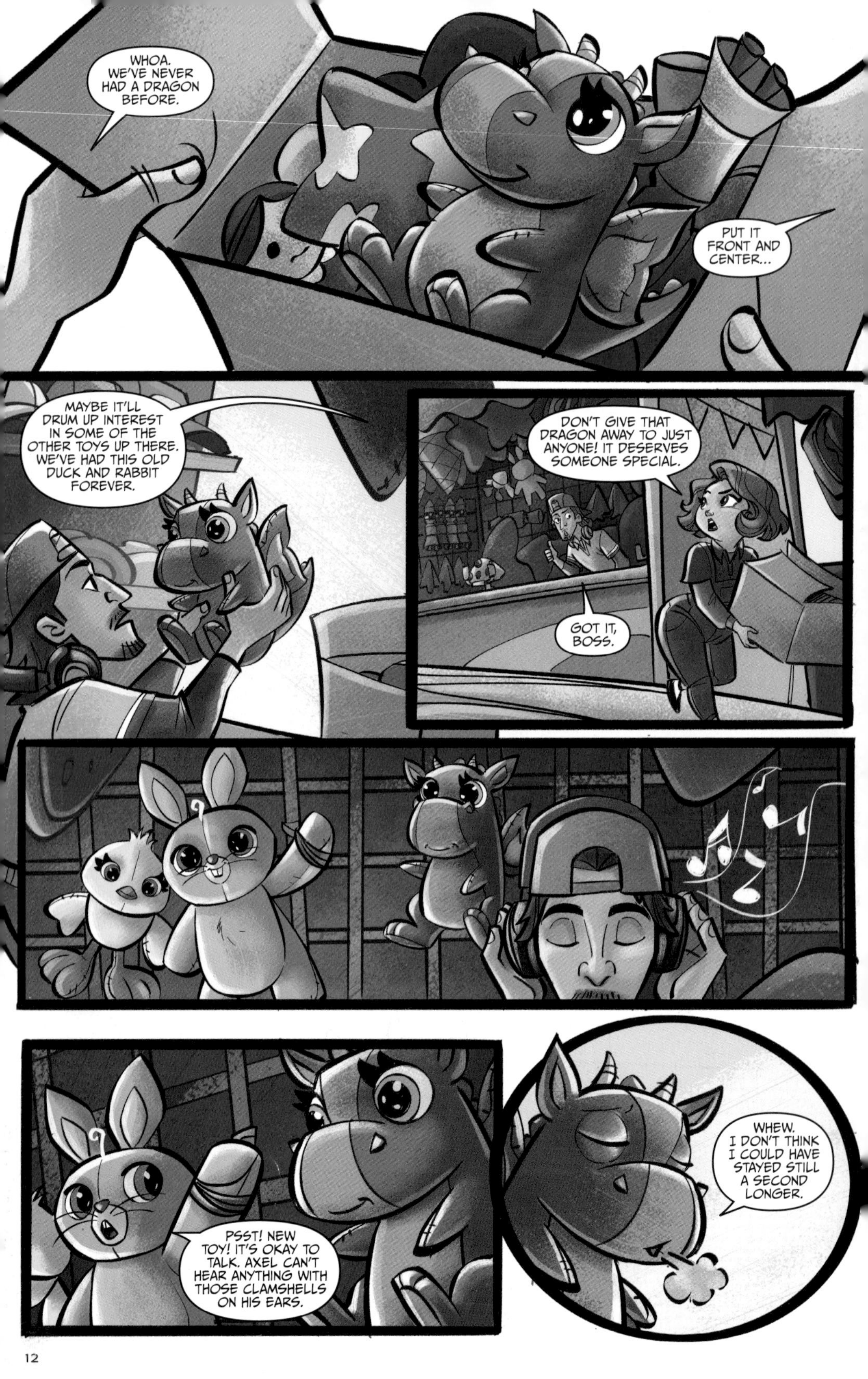
WHOA. WE'VE NEVER HAD A DRAGON BEFORE.
PUT IT FRONT AND CENTER...
MAYBE IT'LL DRUM UP INTEREST IN SOME OF THE OTHER TOYS UP THERE. WE'VE HAD THIS OLD DUCK AND RABBIT FOREVER.
DON'T GIVE THAT DRAGON AWAY TO JUST ANYONE! IT DESERVES SOMEONE SPECIAL.
GOT IT, BOSS.
PSST! NEW TOY! IT'S OKAY TO TALK. AXEL CAN'T HEAR ANYTHING WITH THOSE CLAMSHELLS ON HIS EARS.
WHEW. I DON'T THINK I COULD HAVE STAYED STILL A SECOND LONGER.

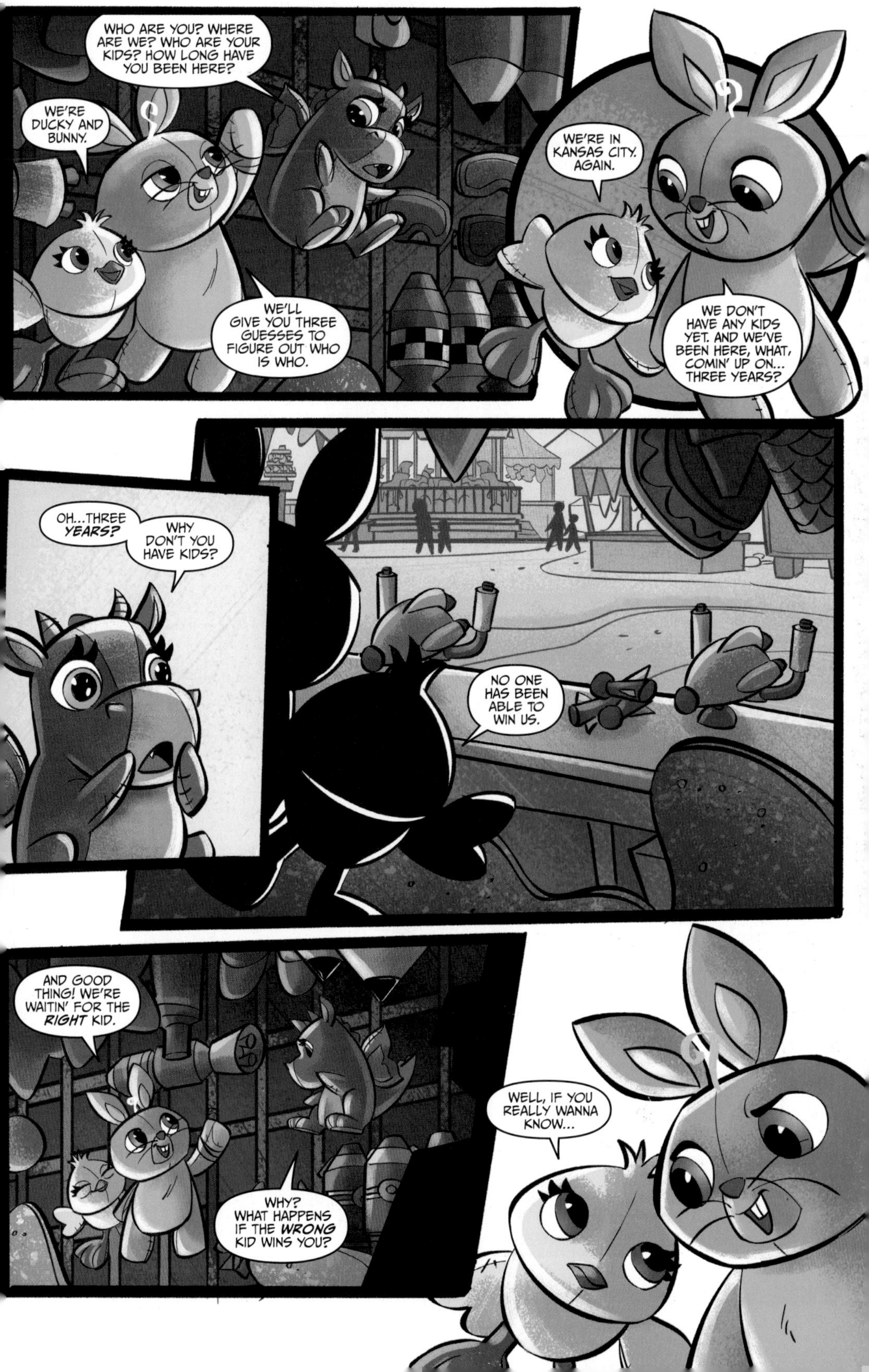
WHO ARE YOU? WHERE ARE WE? WHO ARE YOUR KIDS? HOW LONG HAVE YOU BEEN HERE?
WE'RE DUCKY AND BUNNY.
WE'LL GIVE YOU THREE GUESSES TO FIGURE OUT WHO IS WHO.
WE'RE IN KANSAS CITY. AGAIN.
WE DON'T HAVE ANY KIDS YET. AND WE'VE BEEN HERE, WHAT, COMIN' UP ON... THREE YEARS?
OH...THREE *YEARS?*
WHY DON'T YOU HAVE KIDS?
NO ONE HAS BEEN ABLE TO WIN US.
AND GOOD THING! WE'RE WAITIN' FOR THE *RIGHT* KID.
WHY? WHAT HAPPENS IF THE *WRONG* KID WINS YOU?
WELL, IF YOU REALLY WANNA KNOW...

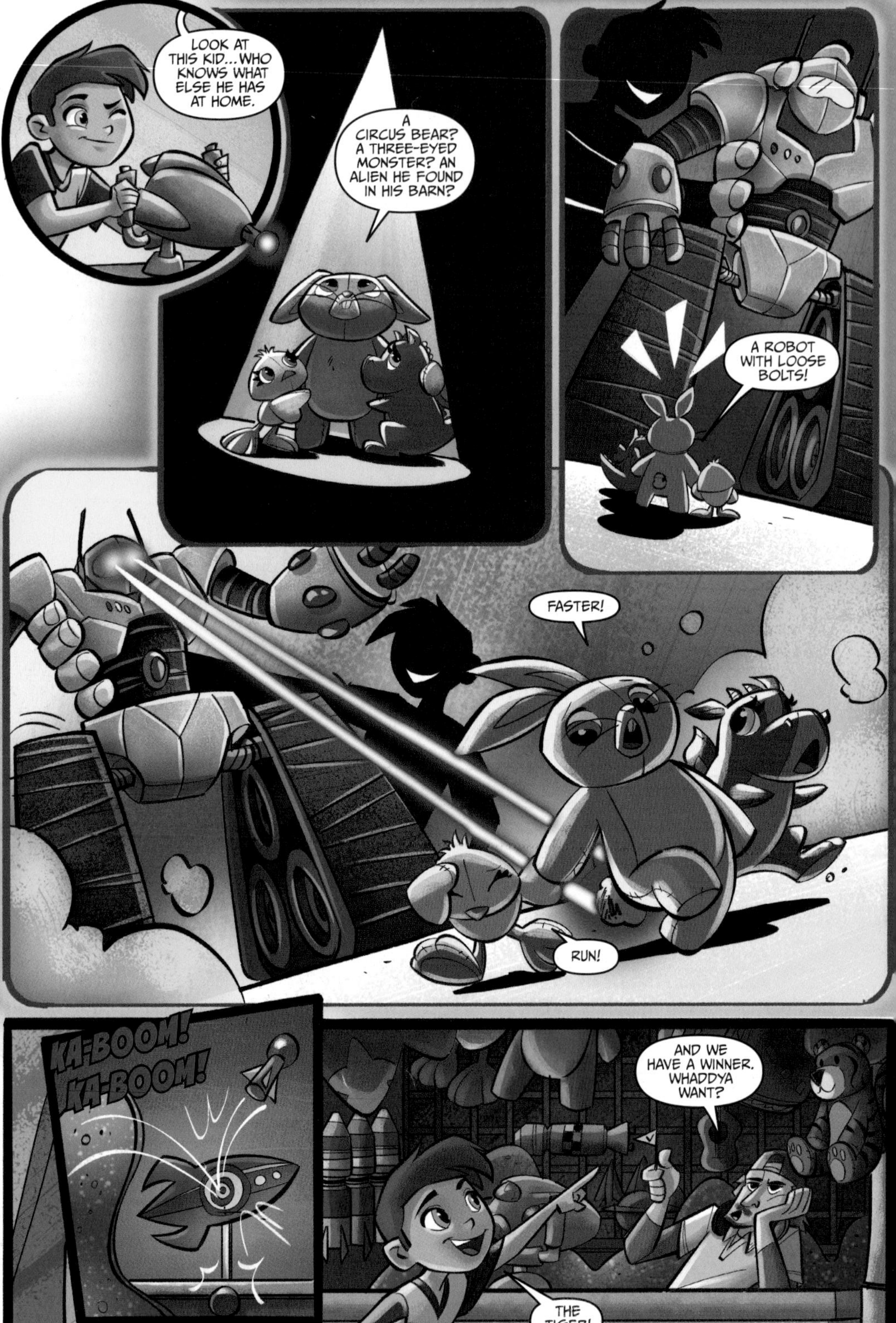
LOOK AT THIS KID...WHO KNOWS WHAT ELSE HE HAS AT HOME.
A CIRCUS BEAR? A THREE-EYED MONSTER? AN ALIEN HE FOUND IN HIS BARN?
A ROBOT WITH LOOSE BOLTS!
FASTER!
RUN!
KA-BOOM! KA-BOOM!
AND WE HAVE A WINNER. WHADDYA WANT?
THE TIGER!

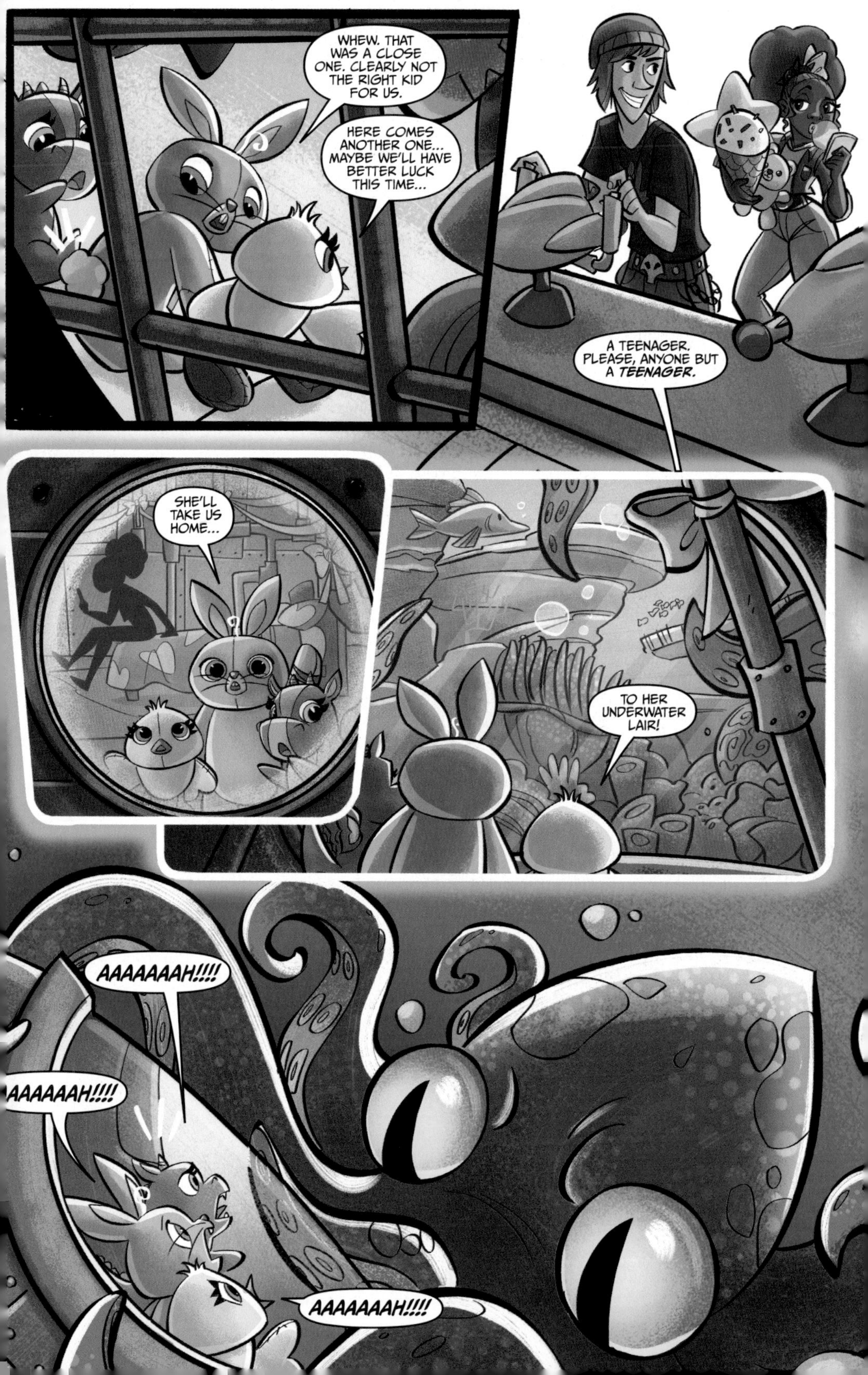
WHEW. THAT WAS A CLOSE ONE. CLEARLY NOT THE RIGHT KID FOR US.
HERE COMES ANOTHER ONE... MAYBE WE'LL HAVE BETTER LUCK THIS TIME...
A TEENAGER. PLEASE, ANYONE BUT A *TEENAGER.*
SHE'LL TAKE US HOME...
TO HER UNDERWATER LAIR!
AAAAAAAH!!!!
AAAAAAH!!!!
AAAAAAAH!!!!

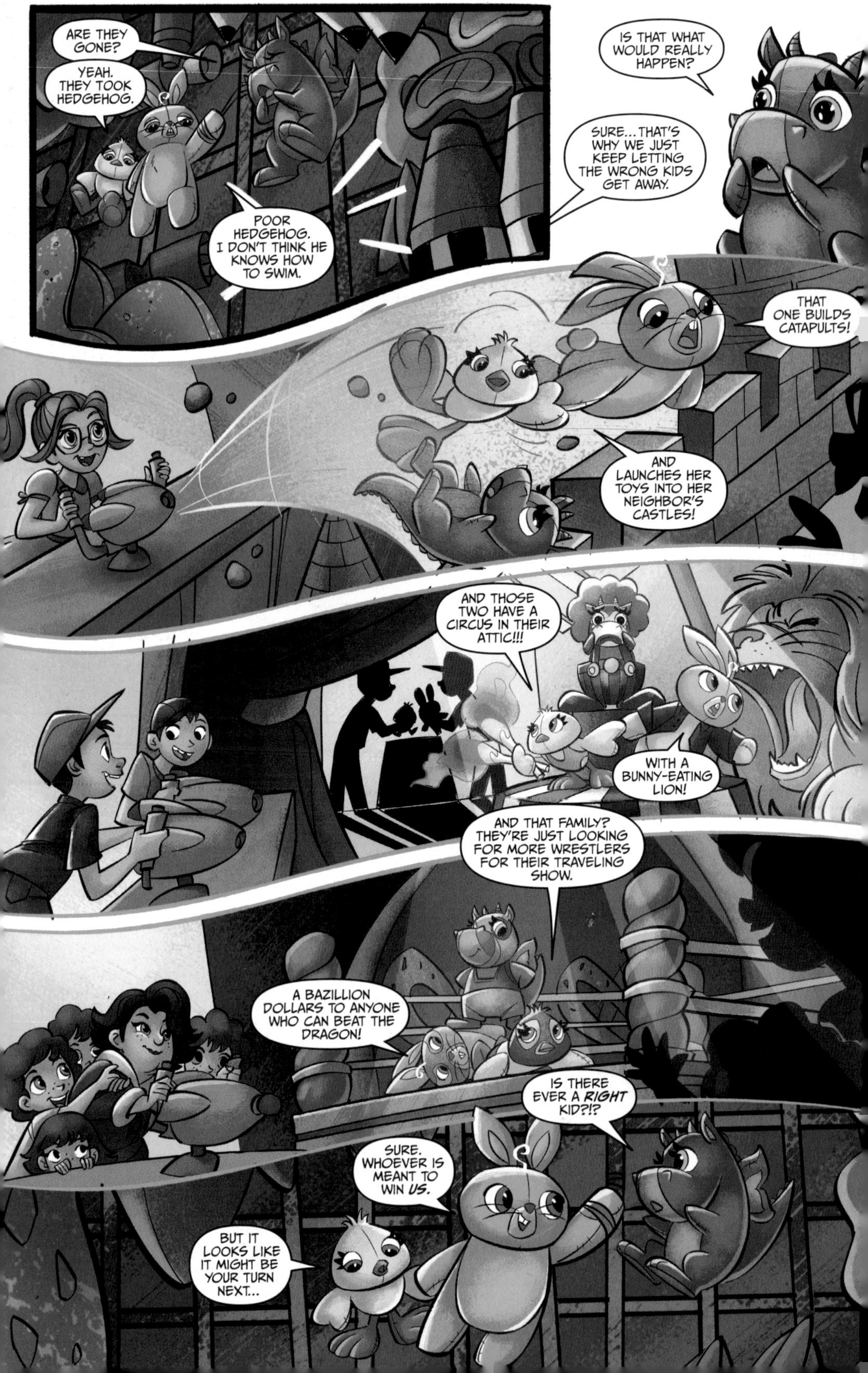
ARE THEY GONE?
YEAH. THEY TOOK HEDGEHOG.
POOR HEDGEHOG. I DON'T THINK HE KNOWS HOW TO SWIM.
IS THAT WHAT WOULD REALLY HAPPEN?
SURE... THAT'S WHY WE JUST KEEP LETTING THE WRONG KIDS GET AWAY.
THAT ONE BUILDS CATAPULTS!
AND LAUNCHES HER TOYS INTO HER NEIGHBOR'S CASTLES!
AND THOSE TWO HAVE A CIRCUS IN THEIR ATTIC!!!
WITH A BUNNY-EATING LION!
AND THAT FAMILY? THEY'RE JUST LOOKING FOR MORE WRESTLERS FOR THEIR TRAVELING SHOW.
A BAZILLION DOLLARS TO ANYONE WHO CAN BEAT THE DRAGON!
IS THERE EVER A *RIGHT* KID?!?
SURE. WHOEVER IS MEANT TO WIN *US.*
BUT IT LOOKS LIKE IT MIGHT BE YOUR TURN NEXT...

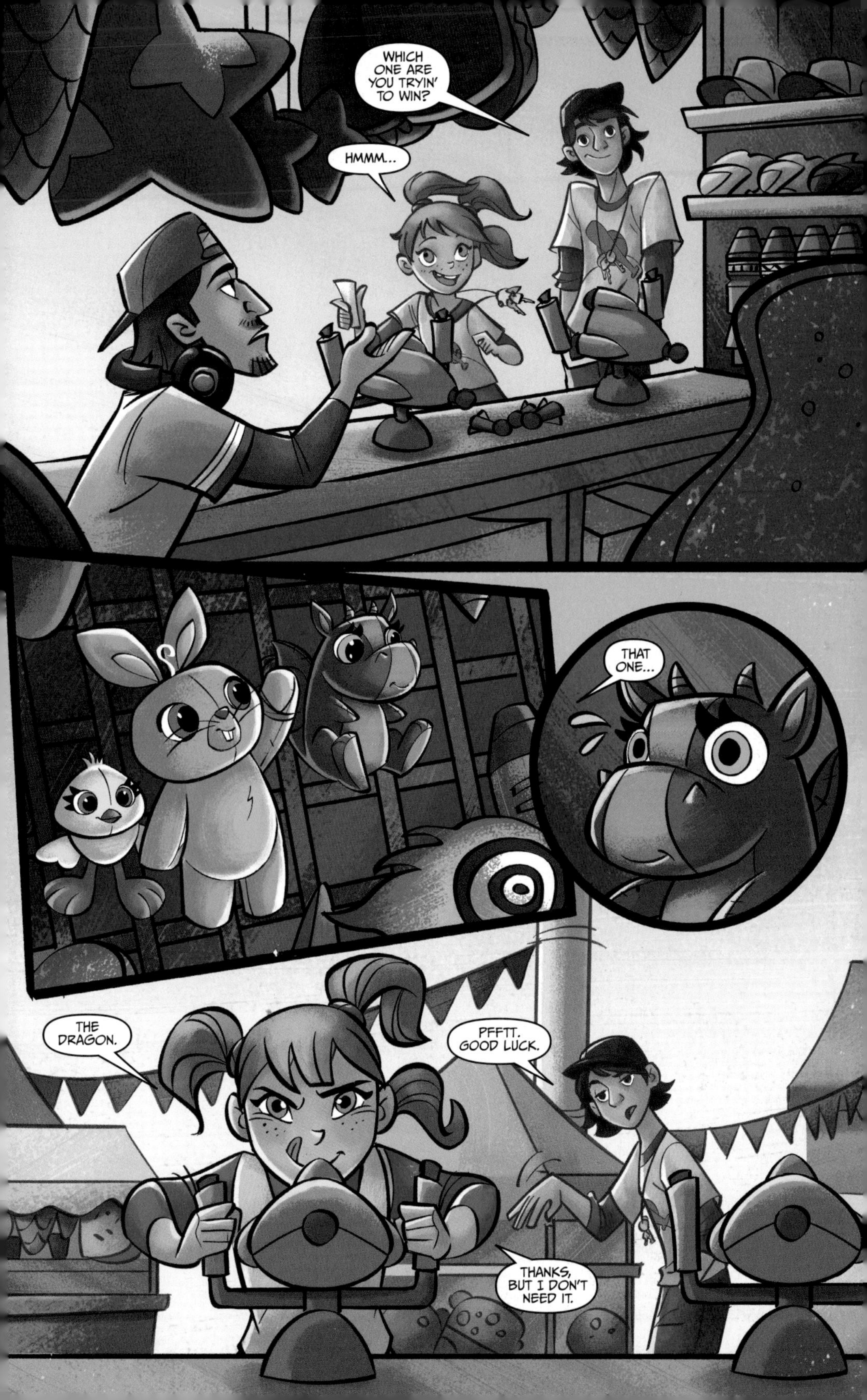
WHICH ONE ARE YOU TRYIN' TO WIN?
HMMM...
THAT ONE...
THE DRAGON.
PFFTT. GOOD LUCK.
THANKS, BUT I DON'T NEED IT.

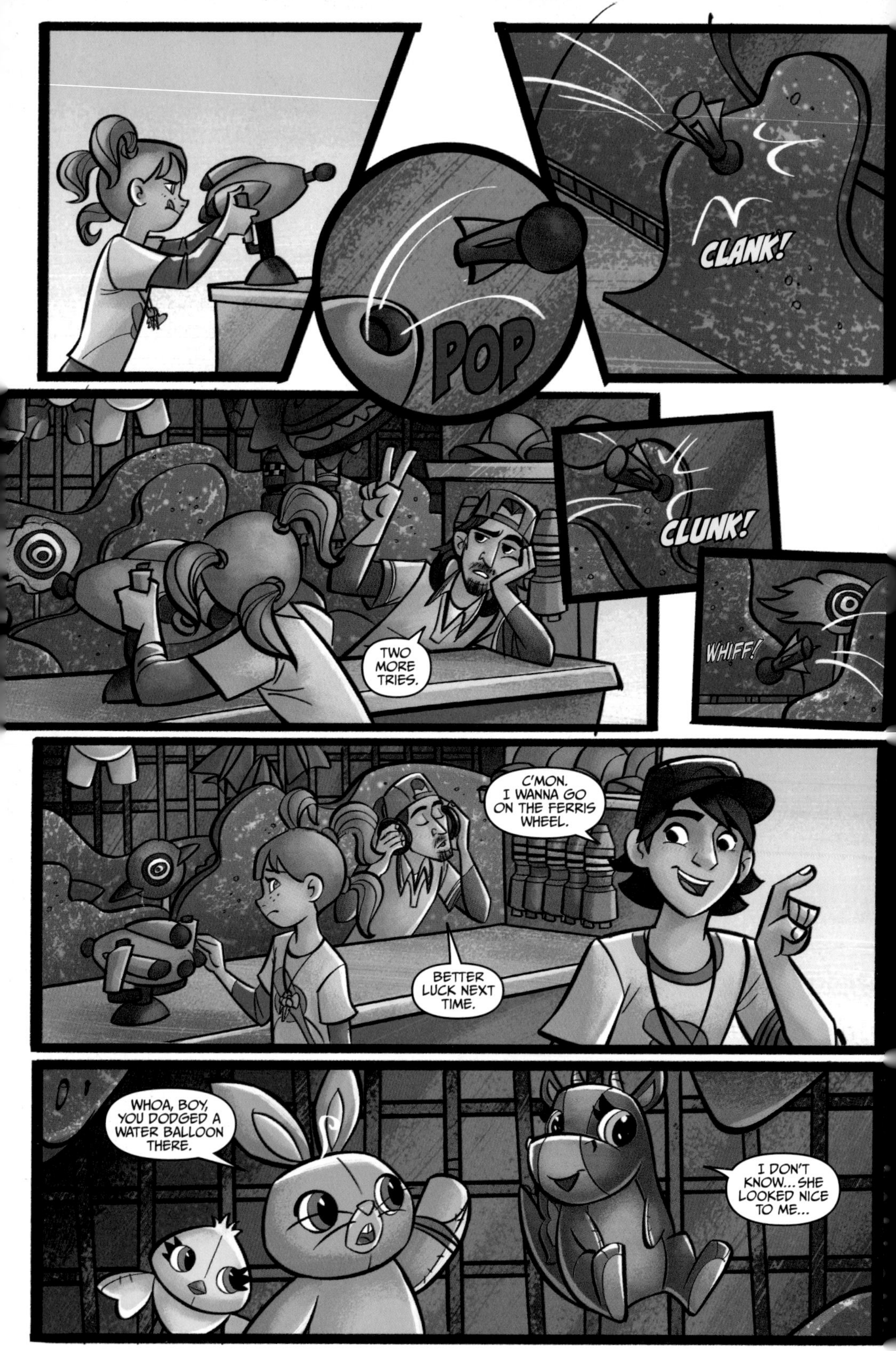
POP
CLANK!
TWO MORE TRIES.
CLUNK!
WHIFF!
C'MON. I WANNA GO ON THE FERRIS WHEEL.
BETTER LUCK NEXT TIME.
WHOA, BOY, YOU DODGED A WATER BALLOON THERE.
I DON'T KNOW... SHE LOOKED NICE TO ME...

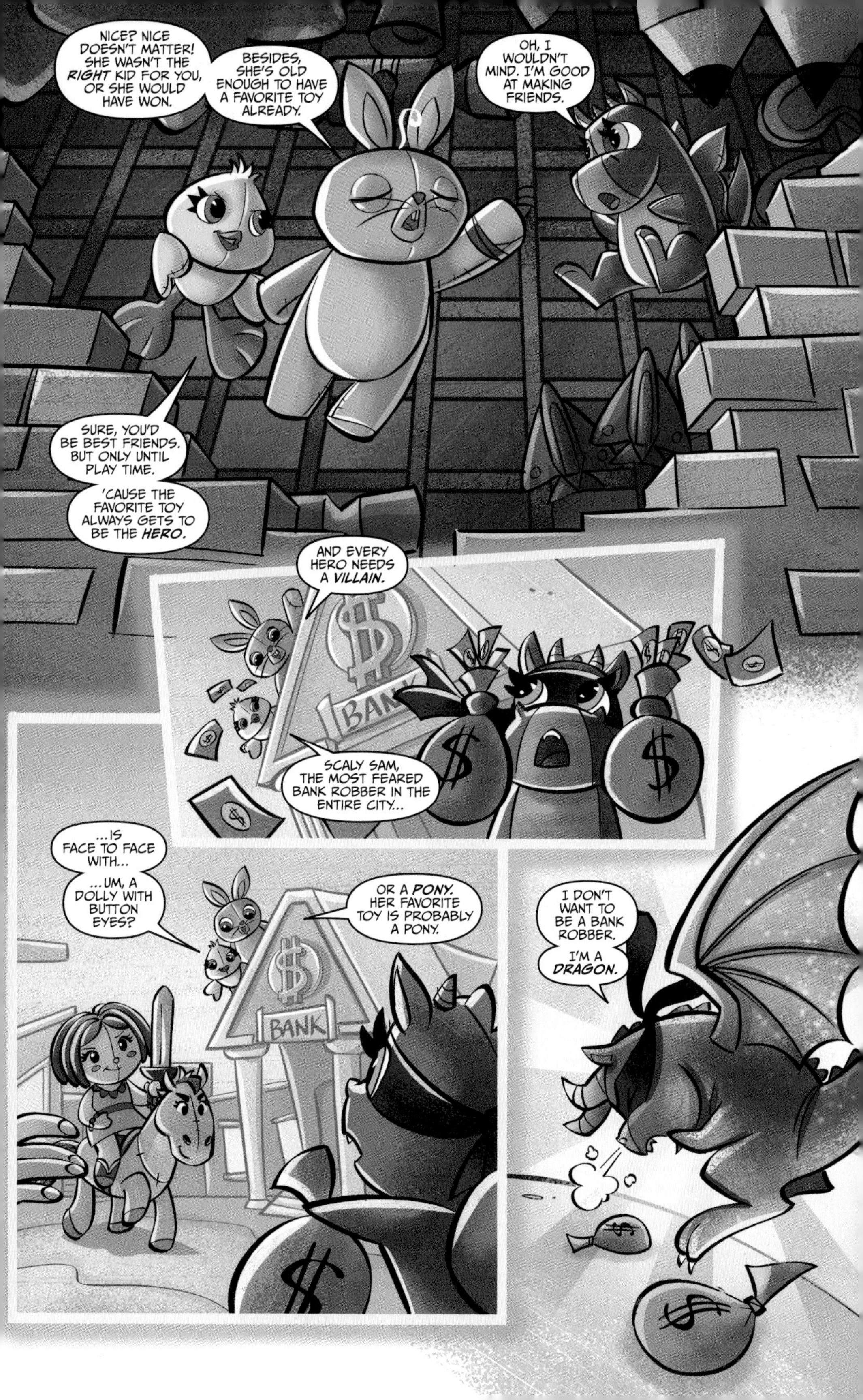
NICE? NICE DOESN'T MATTER! SHE WASN'T THE *RIGHT* KID FOR YOU, OR SHE WOULD HAVE WON.
BESIDES, SHE'S OLD ENOUGH TO HAVE A FAVORITE TOY ALREADY.
OH, I WOULDN'T MIND. I'M GOOD AT MAKING FRIENDS.
SURE, YOU'D BE BEST FRIENDS. BUT ONLY UNTIL PLAY TIME.
'CAUSE THE FAVORITE TOY ALWAYS GETS TO BE THE *HERO.*
AND EVERY HERO NEEDS A *VILLAIN.*
BANK
SCALY SAM, THE MOST FEARED BANK ROBBER IN THE ENTIRE CITY...
...IS FACE TO FACE WITH...
...UM, A DOLLY WITH BUTTON EYES?
OR A *PONY.* HER FAVORITE TOY IS PROBABLY A PONY.
BANK
I DON'T WANT TO BE A BANK ROBBER.
I'M A *DRAGON.*

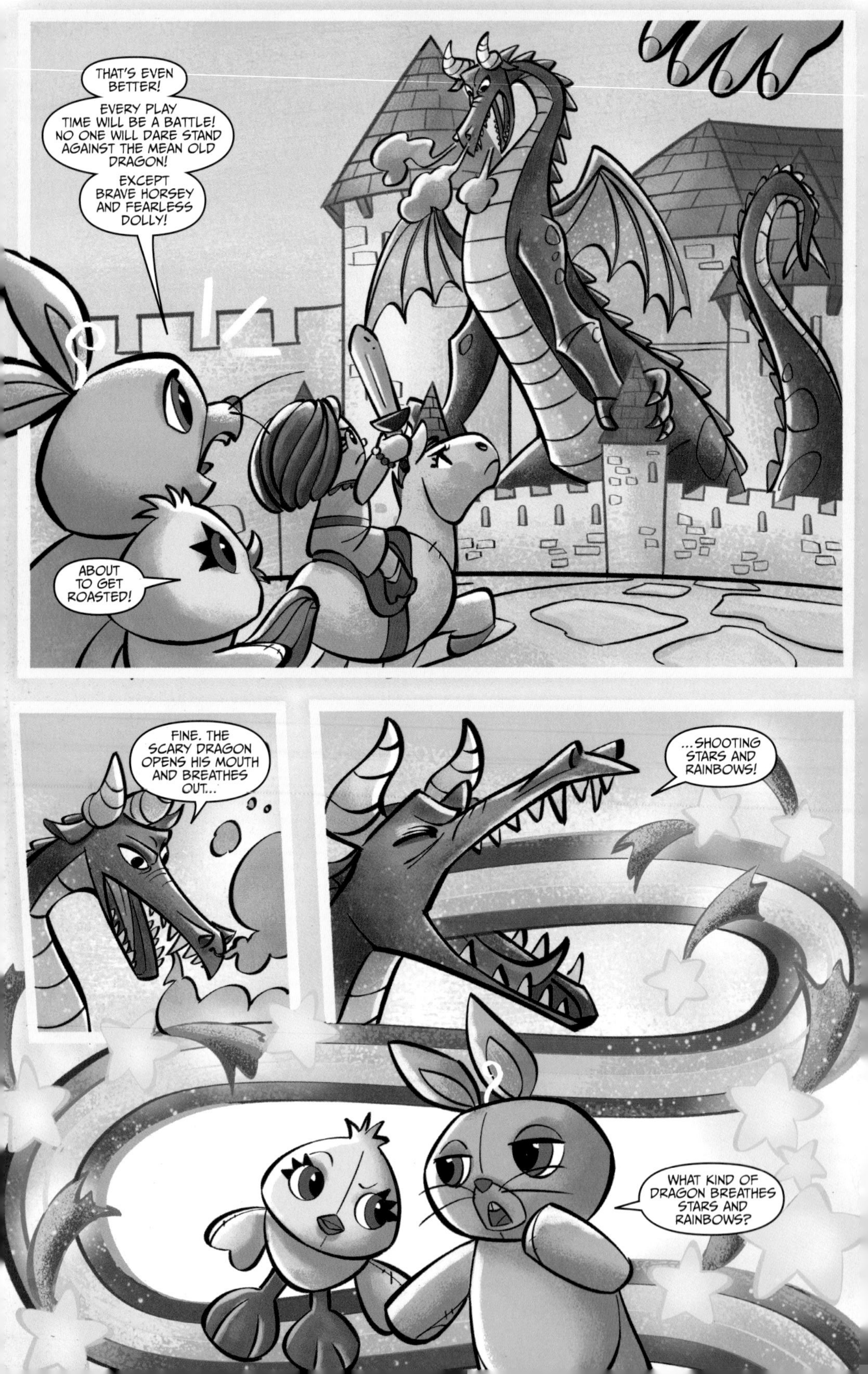
THAT'S EVEN BETTER!
EVERY PLAY TIME WILL BE A BATTLE! NO ONE WILL DARE STAND AGAINST THE MEAN OLD DRAGON!
EXCEPT BRAVE HORSEY AND FEARLESS DOLLY!
ABOUT TO GET ROASTED!
FINE. THE SCARY DRAGON OPENS HIS MOUTH AND BREATHES OUT...
...SHOOTING STARS AND RAINBOWS!
WHAT KIND OF DRAGON BREATHES STARS AND RAINBOWS?

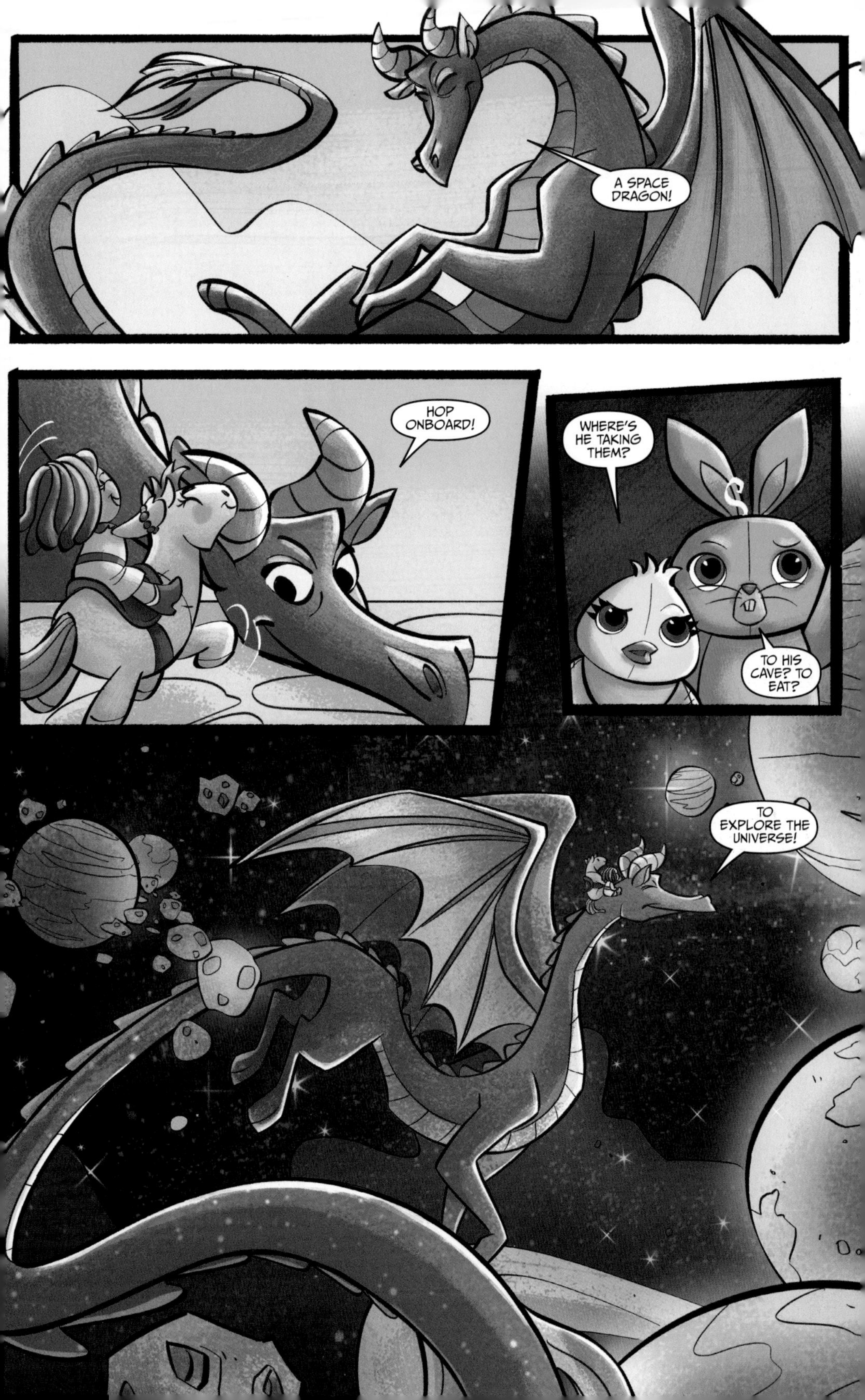
A SPACE DRAGON!
HOP ONBOARD!
WHERE'S HE TAKING THEM?
TO HIS CAVE? TO EAT?
TO EXPLORE THE UNIVERSE!

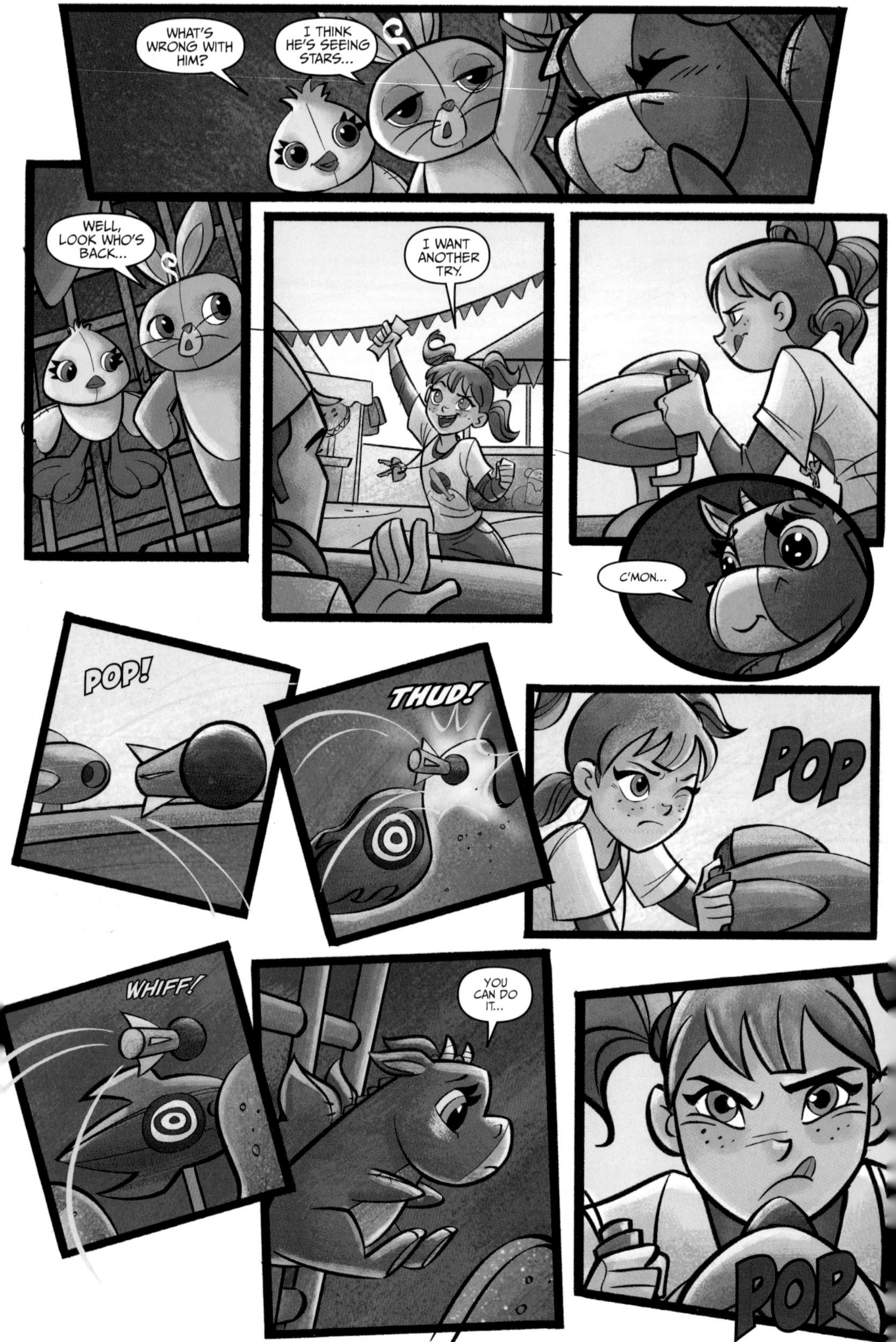
WHAT'S WRONG WITH HIM?
I THINK HE'S SEEING STARS...
WELL, LOOK WHO'S BACK...
I WANT ANOTHER TRY.
C'MON...
POP!
THUD!
POP
WHIFF!
YOU CAN DO IT...
POP

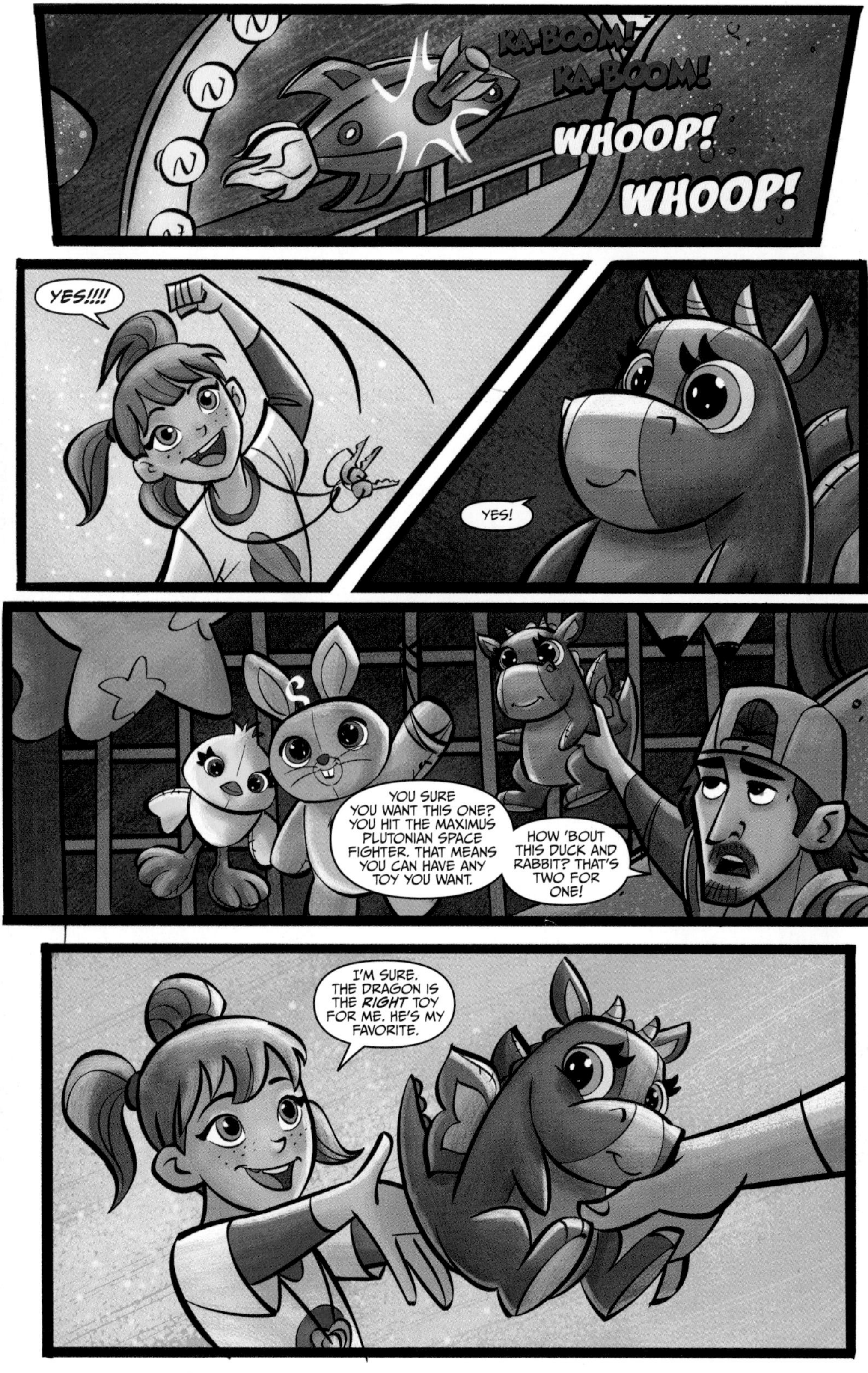
KA-BOOM!
KA-BOOM!
WHOOP!
WHOOP!
YES!!!!
YES!
YOU SURE YOU WANT THIS ONE? YOU HIT THE MAXIMUS PLUTONIAN SPACE FIGHTER. THAT MEANS YOU CAN HAVE ANY TOY YOU WANT.
HOW 'BOUT THIS DUCK AND RABBIT? THAT'S TWO FOR ONE!
I'M SURE. THE DRAGON IS THE *RIGHT* TOY FOR ME. HE'S MY FAVORITE.

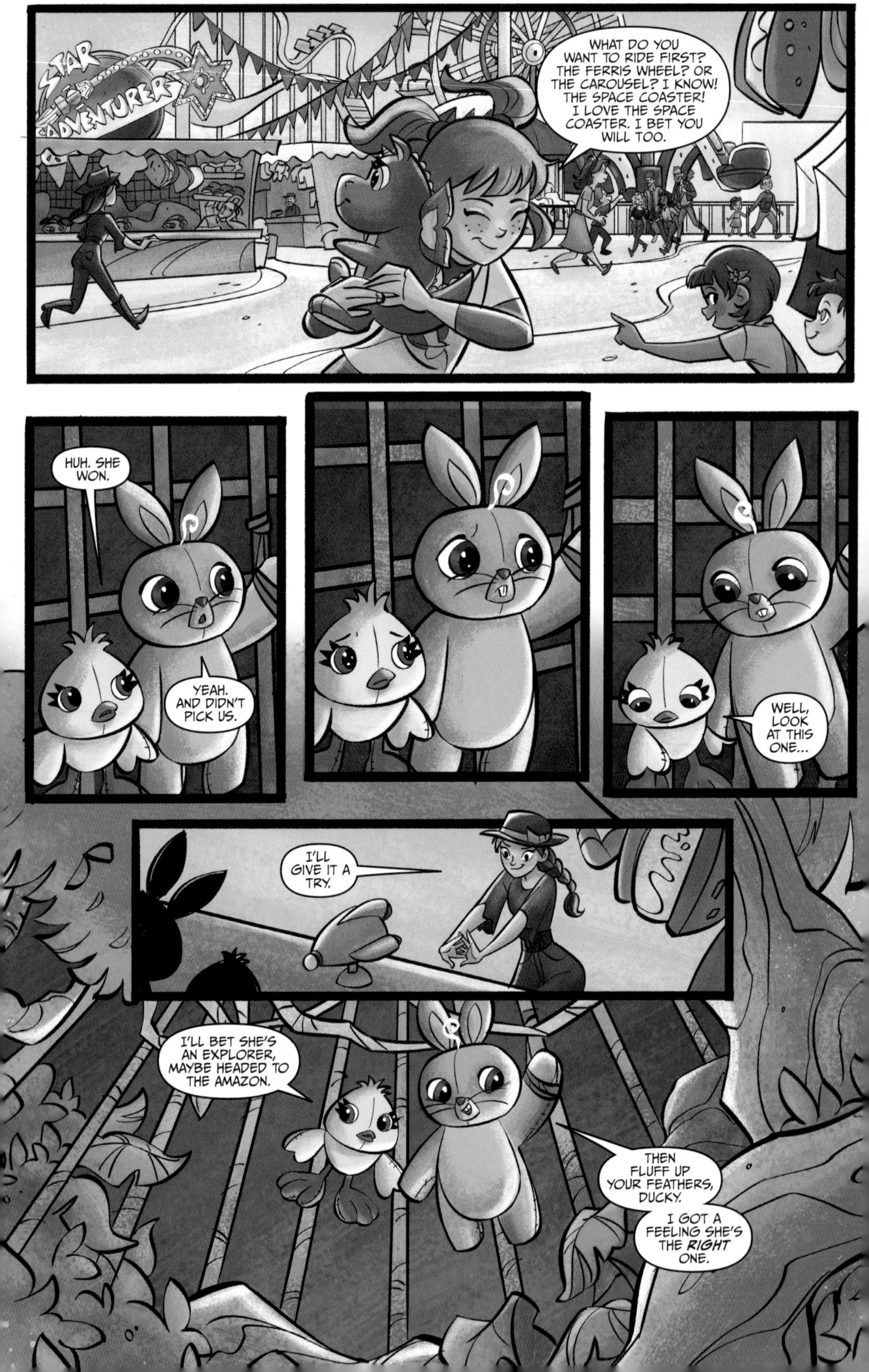
STAR ADVENTURER
WHAT DO YOU WANT TO RIDE FIRST? THE FERRIS WHEEL? OR THE CAROUSEL? I KNOW! THE SPACE COASTER! I LOVE THE SPACE COASTER. I BET YOU WILL TOO.
HUH. SHE WON.
YEAH. AND DIDN'T PICK US.
WELL, LOOK AT THIS ONE...
I'LL GIVE IT A TRY.
I'LL BET SHE'S AN EXPLORER, MAYBE HEADED TO THE AMAZON.
THEN FLUFF UP YOUR FEATHERS, DUCKY.
I GOT A FEELING SHE'S THE *RIGHT* ONE.

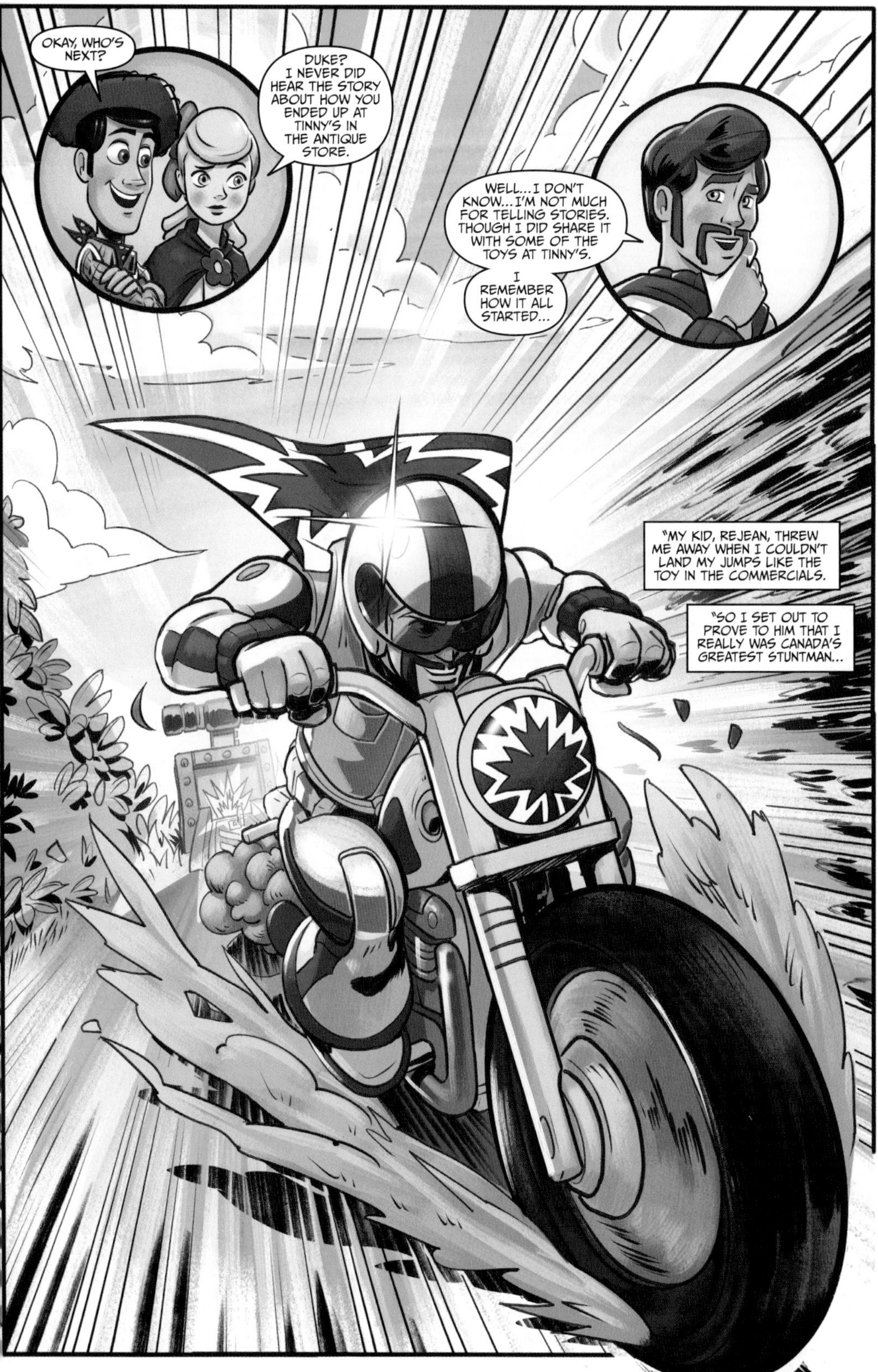

OKAY, WHO'S NEXT?
DUKE? I NEVER DID HEAR THE STORY ABOUT HOW YOU ENDED UP AT TINNY'S IN THE ANTIQUE STORE.
WELL...I DON'T KNOW...I'M NOT MUCH FOR TELLING STORIES. THOUGH I DID SHARE IT WITH SOME OF THE TOYS AT TINNY'S.
I REMEMBER HOW IT ALL STARTED...
"MY KID, REJEAN, THREW ME AWAY WHEN I COULDN'T LAND MY JUMPS LIKE THE TOY IN THE COMMERCIALS.
"SO I SET OUT TO PROVE TO HIM THAT I REALLY WAS CANADA'S GREATEST STUNTMAN...

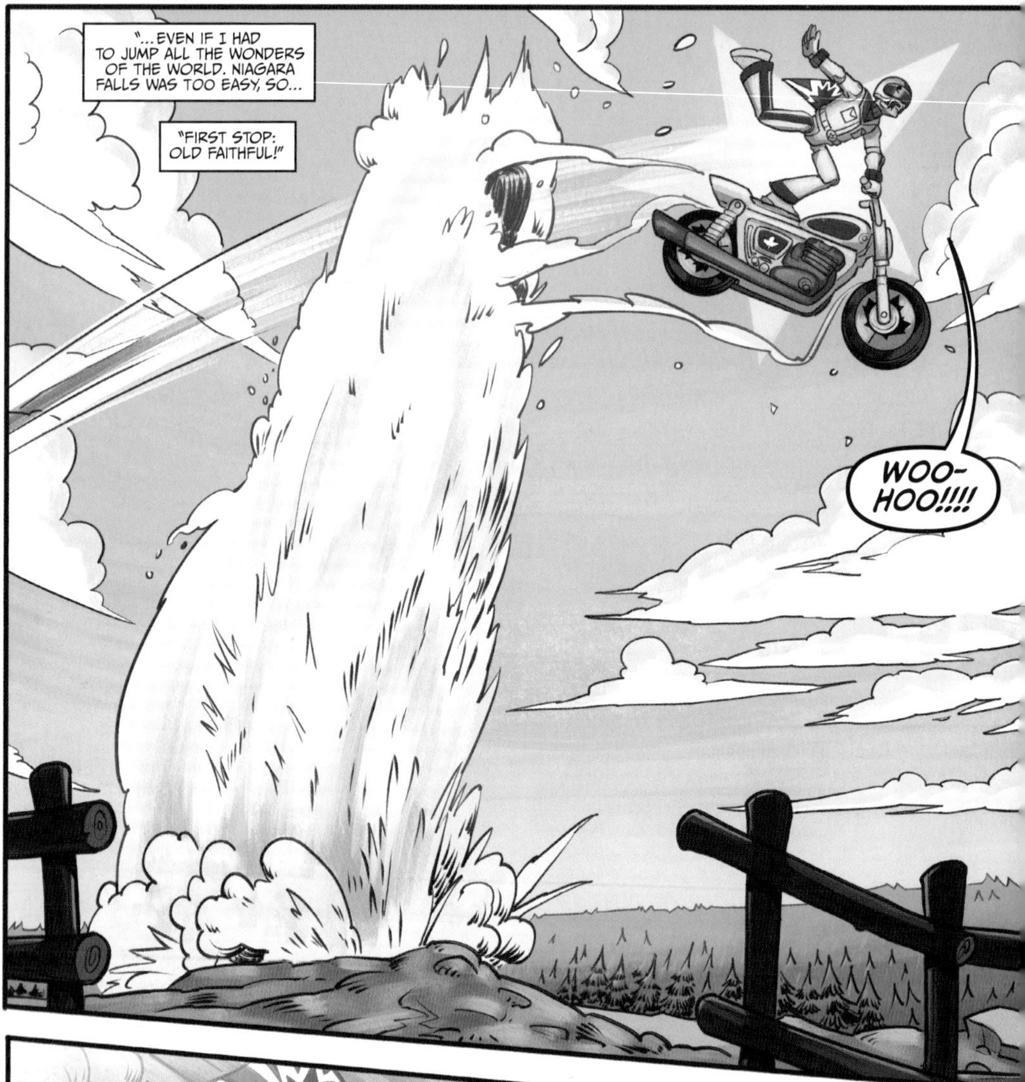
"...EVEN IF I HAD TO JUMP ALL THE WONDERS OF THE WORLD. NIAGARA FALLS WAS TOO EASY, SO...
"FIRST STOP: OLD FAITHFUL!"
WOO-HOO!!!!

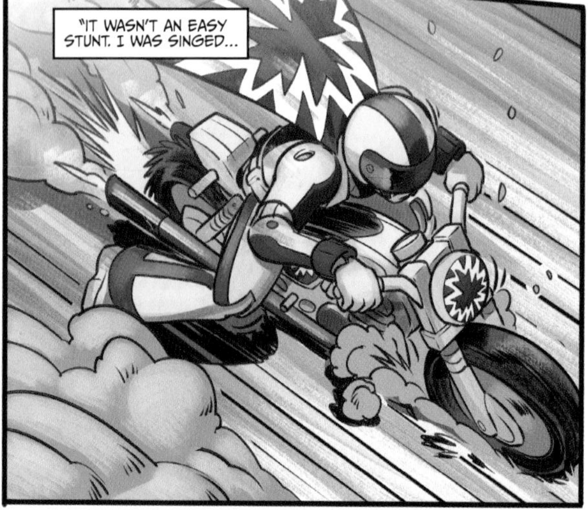
"IT WASN'T AN EASY STUNT. I WAS SINGED...

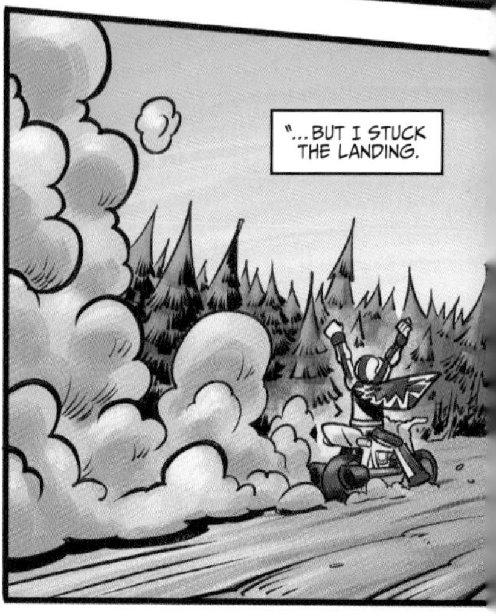
"...BUT I STUCK THE LANDING.

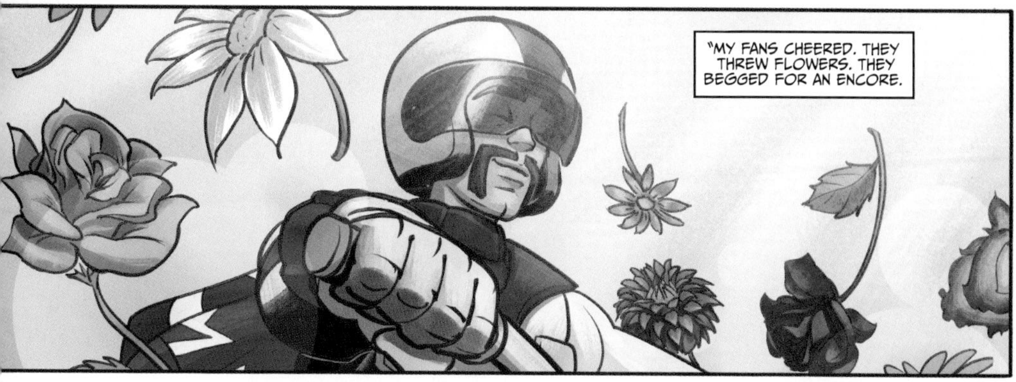
"MY FANS CHEERED. THEY THREW FLOWERS. THEY BEGGED FOR AN ENCORE.

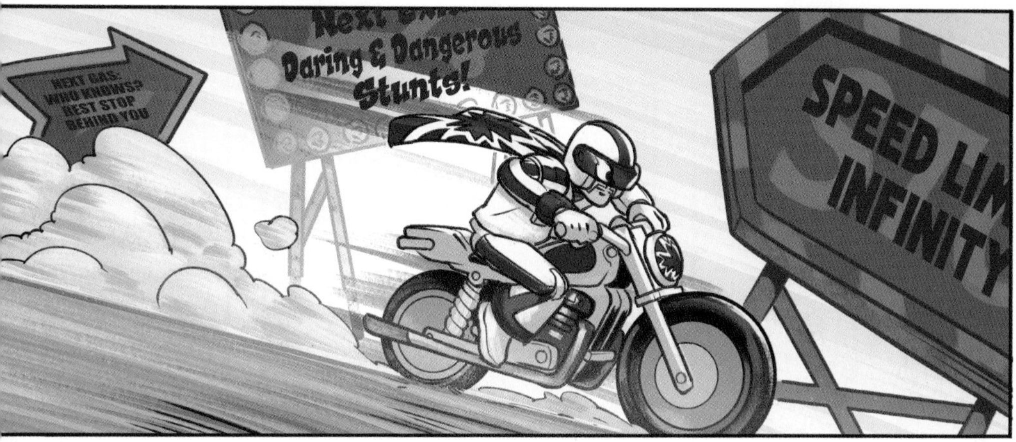
NEXT GAS: WHO KNOWS? REST STOP BEHIND YOU
Daring & Dangerous Stunts!
SPEED LIM
INFINITY

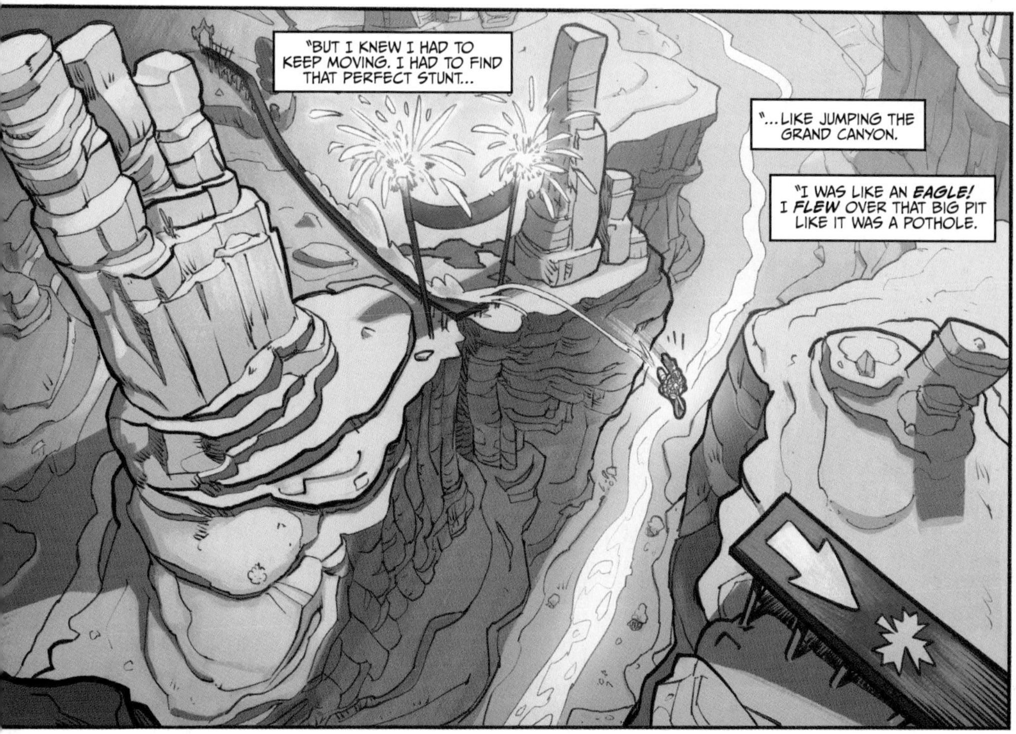
"BUT I KNEW I HAD TO KEEP MOVING. I HAD TO FIND THAT PERFECT STUNT...
"...LIKE JUMPING THE GRAND CANYON.
"I WAS LIKE AN ***EAGLE!*** I ***FLEW*** OVER THAT BIG PIT LIKE IT WAS A POTHOLE.

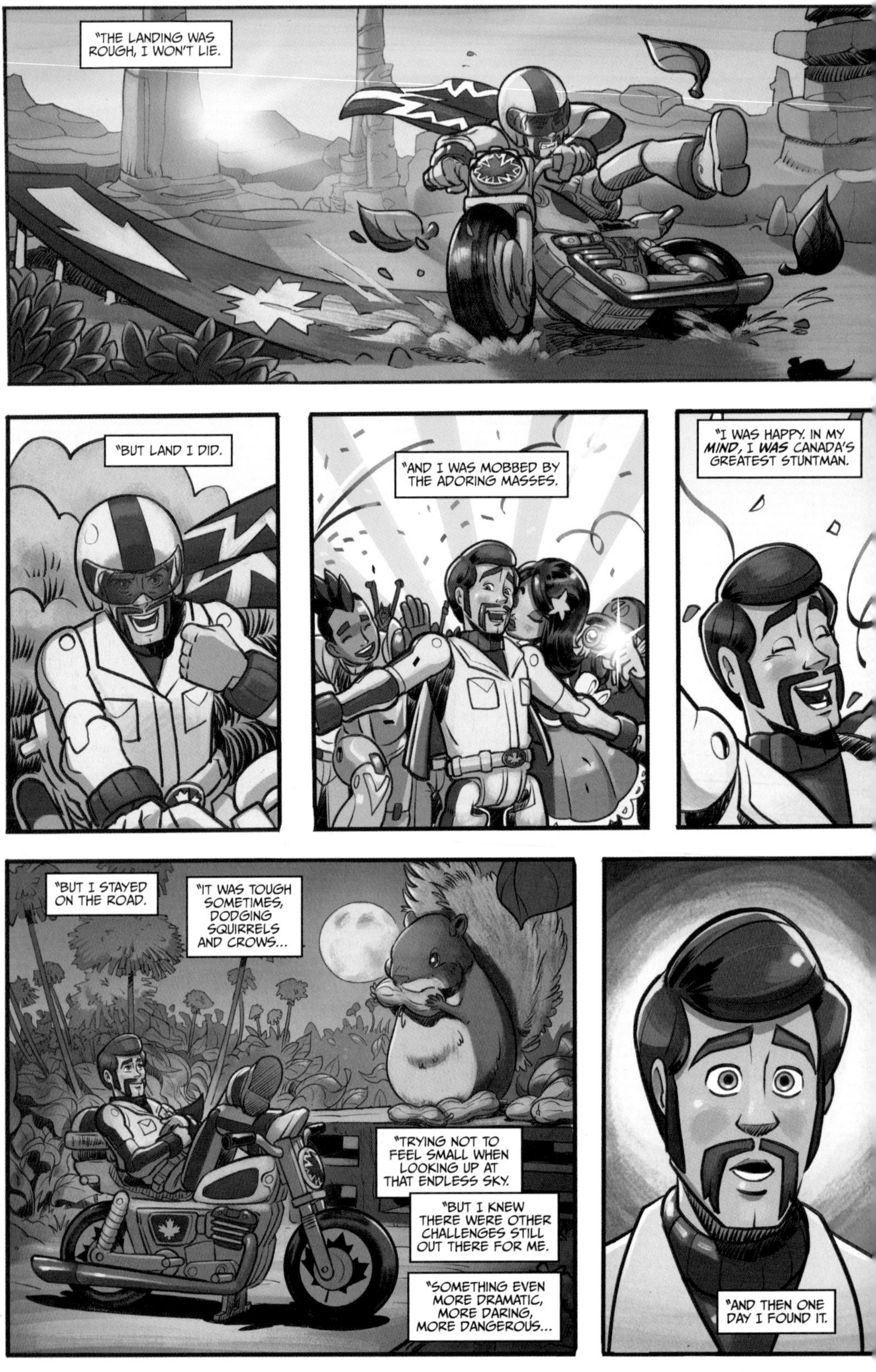
"THE LANDING WAS ROUGH, I WON'T LIE.
"BUT LAND I DID.
"AND I WAS MOBBED BY THE ADORING MASSES.
"I WAS HAPPY. IN MY *MIND*, I *WAS* CANADA'S GREATEST STUNTMAN.
"BUT I STAYED ON THE ROAD.
"IT WAS TOUGH SOMETIMES, DODGING SQUIRRELS AND CROWS...
"TRYING NOT TO FEEL SMALL WHEN LOOKING UP AT THAT ENDLESS SKY.
"BUT I KNEW THERE WERE OTHER CHALLENGES STILL OUT THERE FOR ME.
"SOMETHING EVEN MORE DRAMATIC, MORE DARING, MORE DANGEROUS...
"AND THEN ONE DAY I FOUND IT.

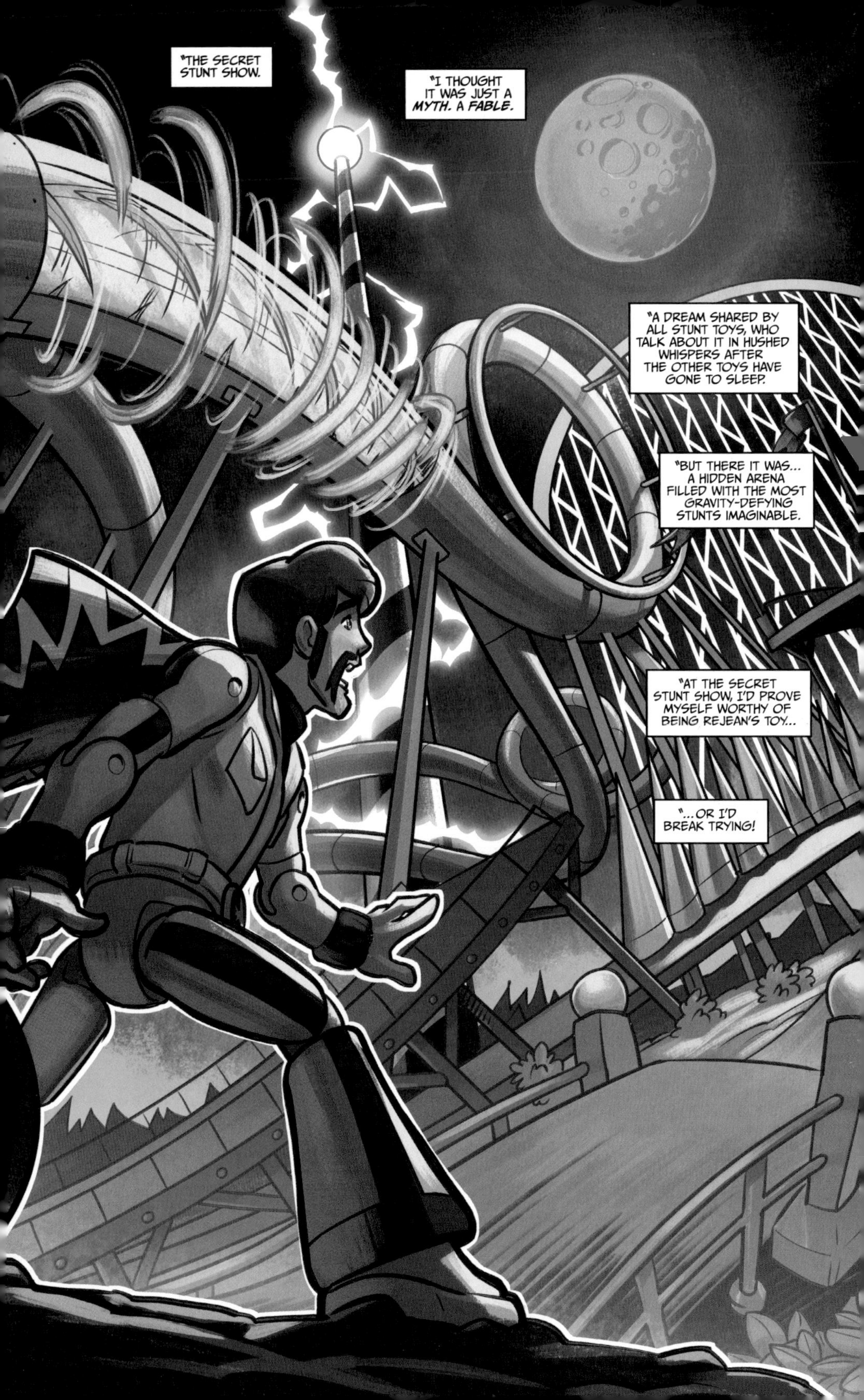
"THE SECRET STUNT SHOW.
"I THOUGHT IT WAS JUST A *MYTH*. A *FABLE*.
"A DREAM SHARED BY ALL STUNT TOYS, WHO TALK ABOUT IT IN HUSHED WHISPERS AFTER THE OTHER TOYS HAVE GONE TO SLEEP.
"BUT THERE IT WAS... A HIDDEN ARENA FILLED WITH THE MOST GRAVITY-DEFYING STUNTS IMAGINABLE.
"AT THE SECRET STUNT SHOW, I'D PROVE MYSELF WORTHY OF BEING REJEAN'S TOY...
"...OR I'D BREAK TRYING!

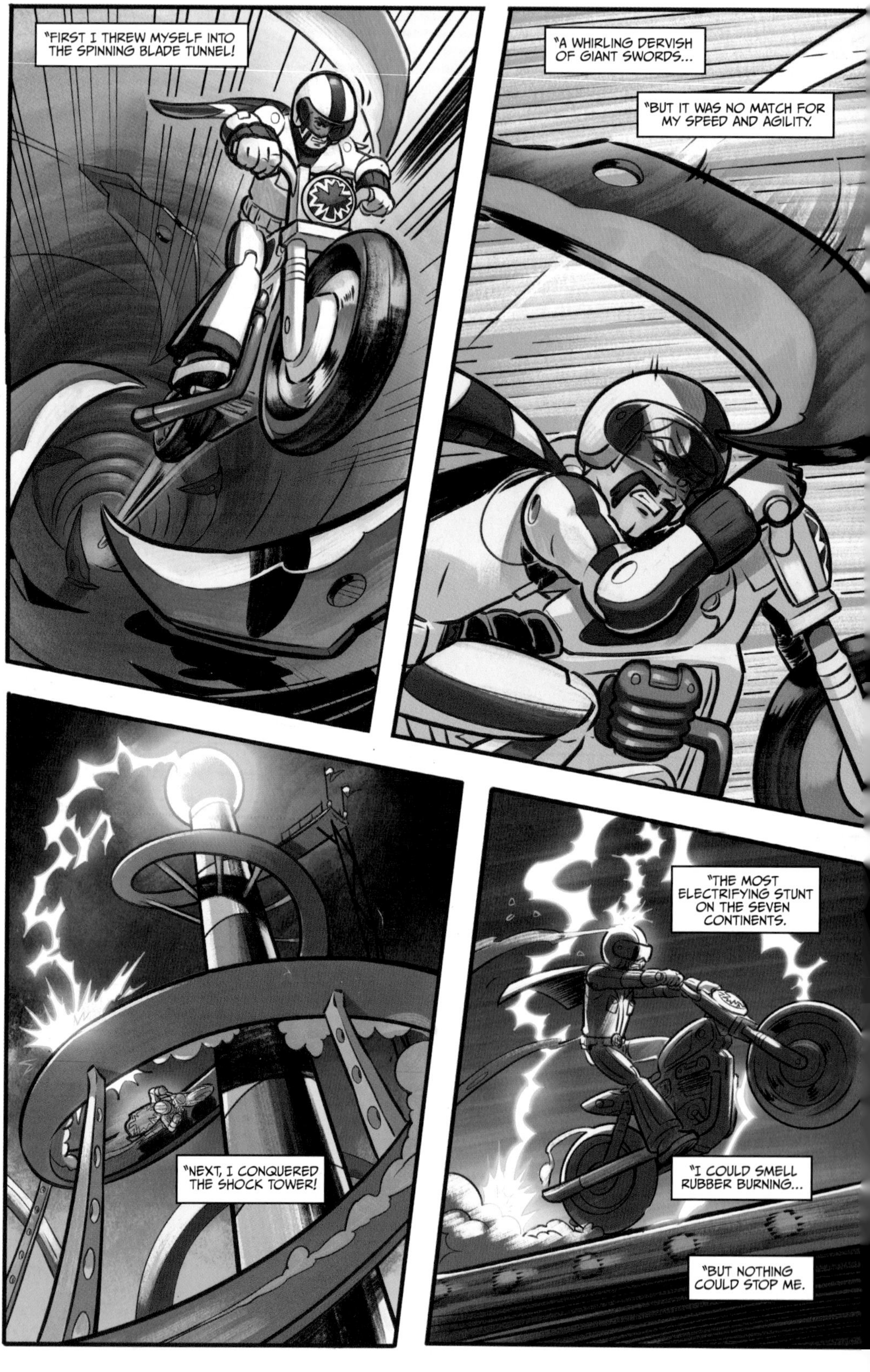
"FIRST I THREW MYSELF INTO THE SPINNING BLADE TUNNEL!
"A WHIRLING DERVISH OF GIANT SWORDS...
"BUT IT WAS NO MATCH FOR MY SPEED AND AGILITY.
"NEXT, I CONQUERED THE SHOCK TOWER!
"THE MOST ELECTRIFYING STUNT ON THE SEVEN CONTINENTS.
"I COULD SMELL RUBBER BURNING...
"BUT NOTHING COULD STOP ME.

"AND FOR MY GRAND FINALE, I BRAVED WHAT OTHER TOYS FEARED MOST...

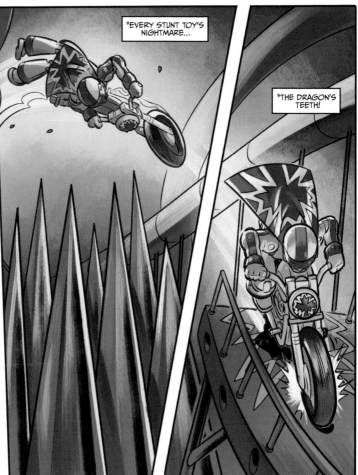

"EVERY STUNT TOY'S NIGHTMARE...

"THE DRAGON'S TEETH!

"THE CROWD ROARED. FLASHBULBS POPPED.

"THE MAYOR GAVE ME THE KEY TO THE CITY.

"I HAD DONE IT. I HAD SURVIVED THE MOST DANGEROUS STUNTS.

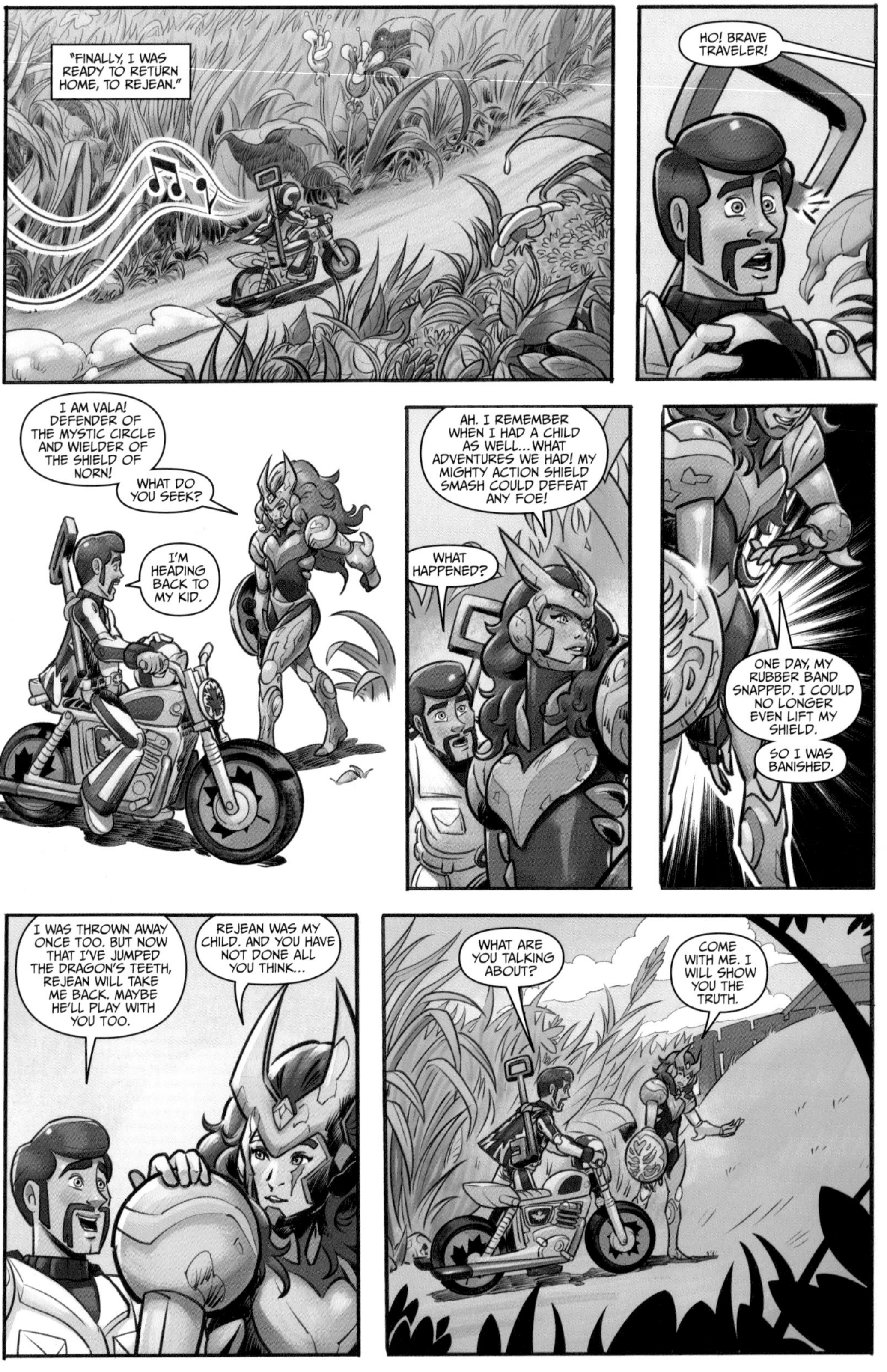
"FINALLY, I WAS READY TO RETURN HOME, TO REJEAN."
HO! BRAVE TRAVELER!
I AM VALA! DEFENDER OF THE MYSTIC CIRCLE AND WIELDER OF THE SHIELD OF NORN!
WHAT DO YOU SEEK?
I'M HEADING BACK TO MY KID.
AH. I REMEMBER WHEN I HAD A CHILD AS WELL...WHAT ADVENTURES WE HAD! MY MIGHTY ACTION SHIELD SMASH COULD DEFEAT ANY FOE!
WHAT HAPPENED?
ONE DAY, MY RUBBER BAND SNAPPED. I COULD NO LONGER EVEN LIFT MY SHIELD.
SO I WAS BANISHED.
I WAS THROWN AWAY ONCE TOO. BUT NOW THAT I'VE JUMPED THE DRAGON'S TEETH, REJEAN WILL TAKE ME BACK. MAYBE HE'LL PLAY WITH YOU TOO.
REJEAN WAS MY CHILD. AND YOU HAVE NOT DONE ALL YOU THINK...
WHAT ARE YOU TALKING ABOUT?
COME WITH ME. I WILL SHOW YOU THE TRUTH.

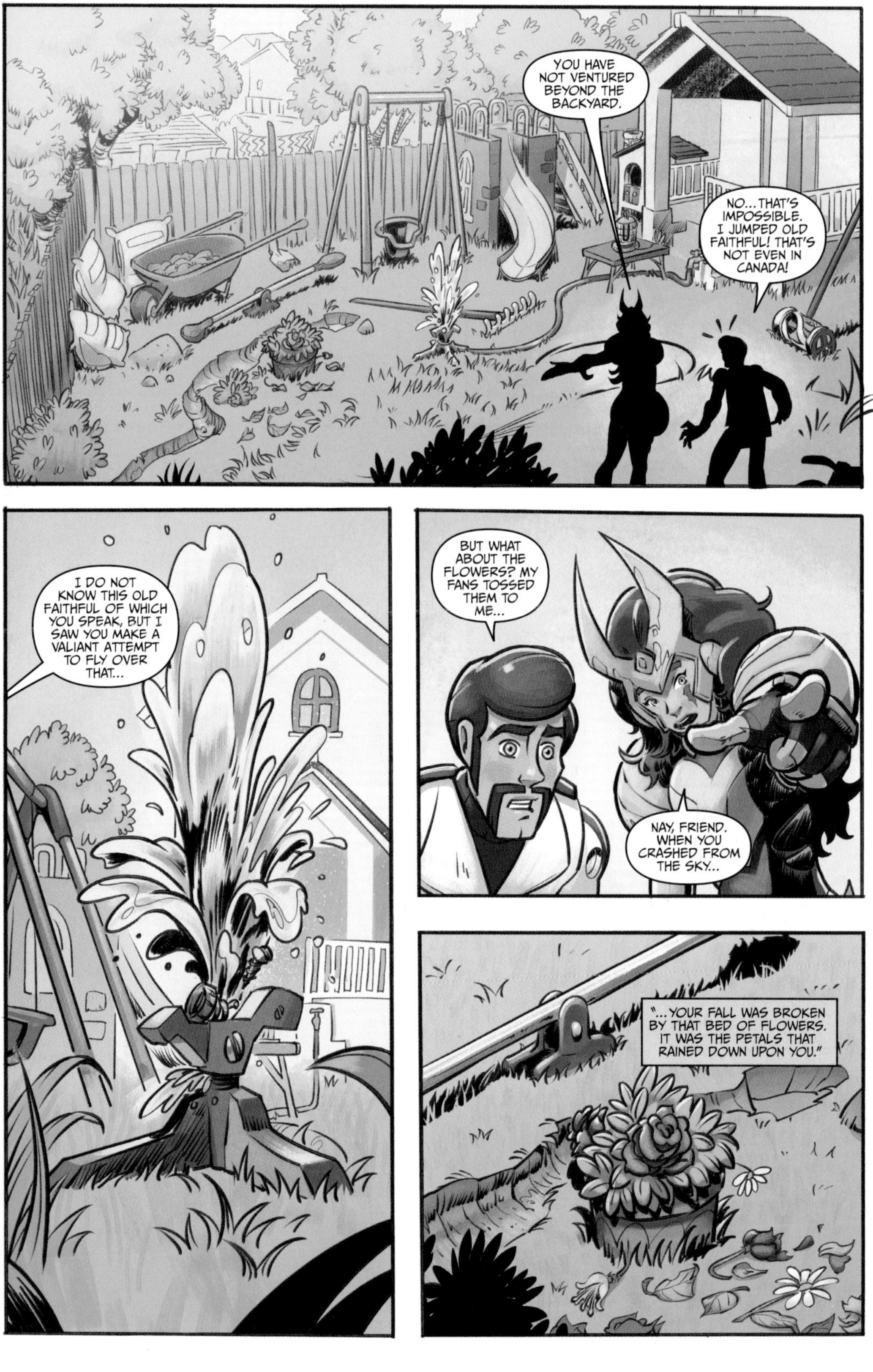
YOU HAVE NOT VENTURED BEYOND THE BACKYARD.
NO... THAT'S IMPOSSIBLE. I JUMPED OLD FAITHFUL! THAT'S NOT EVEN IN CANADA!
I DO NOT KNOW THIS OLD FAITHFUL OF WHICH YOU SPEAK, BUT I SAW YOU MAKE A VALIANT ATTEMPT TO FLY OVER THAT...
BUT WHAT ABOUT THE FLOWERS? MY FANS TOSSED THEM TO ME...
NAY, FRIEND. WHEN YOU CRASHED FROM THE SKY...
"...YOUR FALL WAS BROKEN BY THAT BED OF FLOWERS. IT WAS THE PETALS THAT RAINED DOWN UPON YOU."

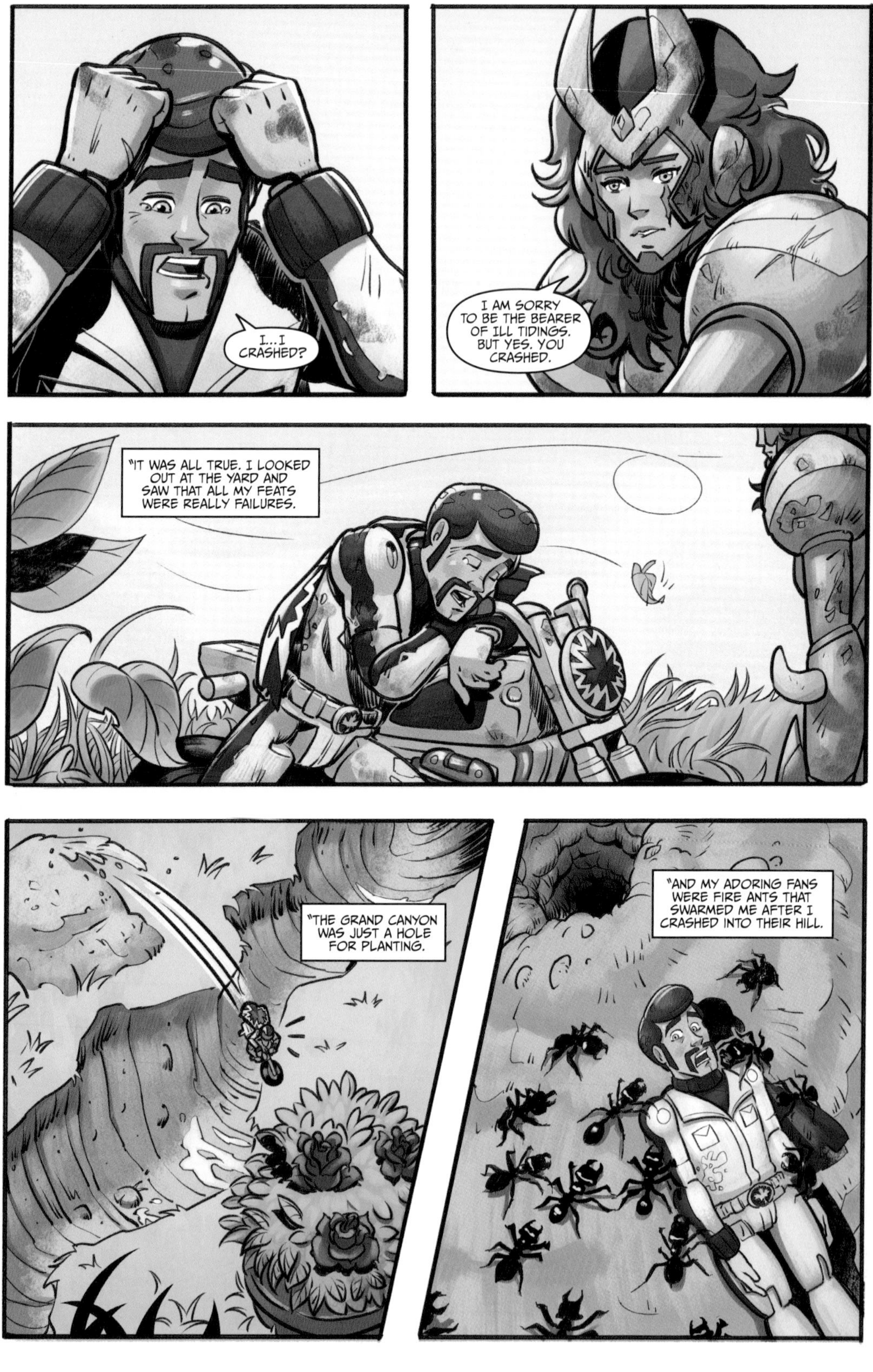
I...I CRASHED?
I AM SORRY TO BE THE BEARER OF ILL TIDINGS. BUT YES. YOU CRASHED.
"IT WAS ALL TRUE. I LOOKED OUT AT THE YARD AND SAW THAT ALL MY FEATS WERE REALLY FAILURES.
"THE GRAND CANYON WAS JUST A HOLE FOR PLANTING.
"AND MY ADORING FANS WERE FIRE ANTS THAT SWARMED ME AFTER I CRASHED INTO THEIR HILL.

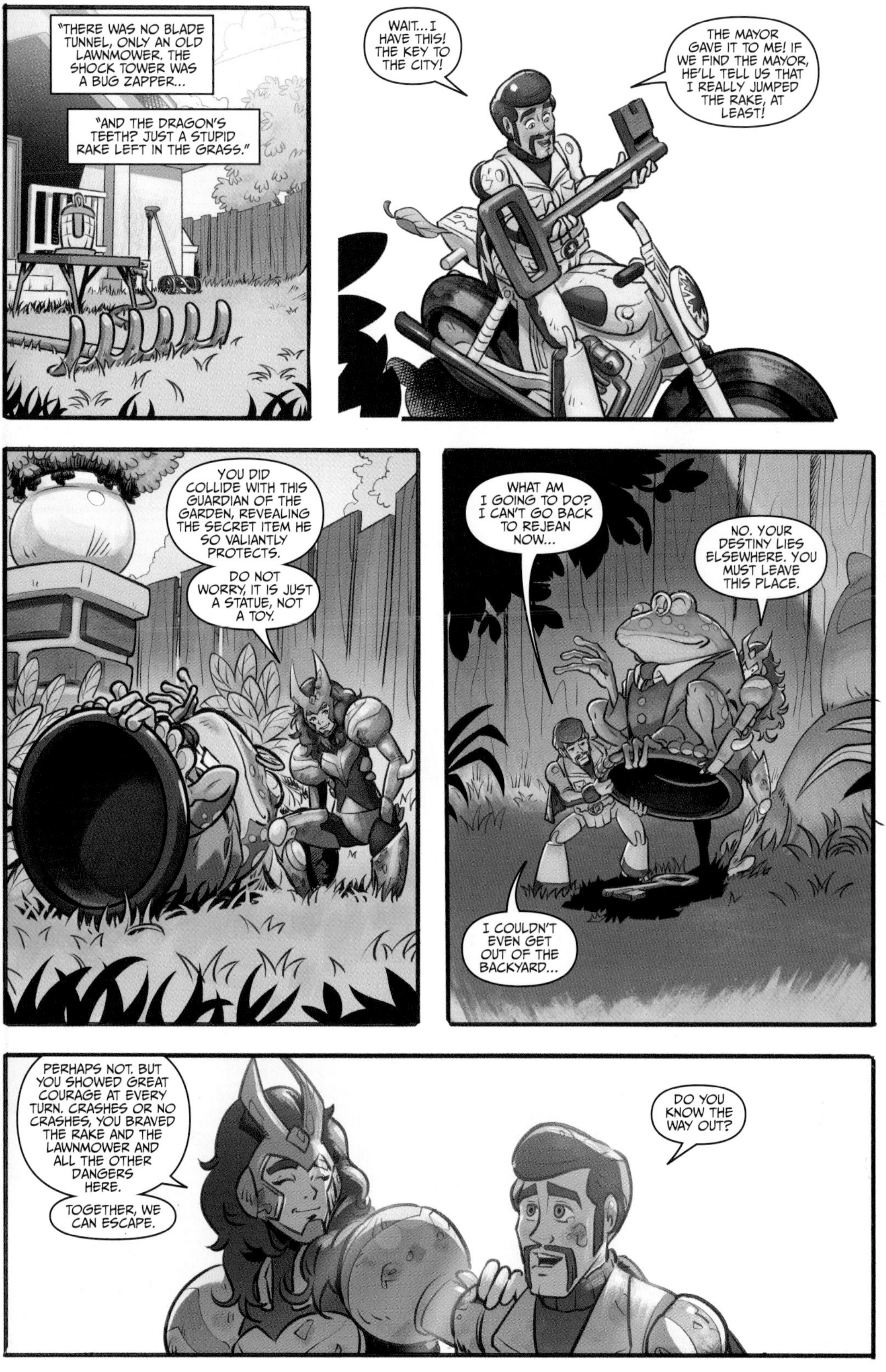
"THERE WAS NO BLADE TUNNEL, ONLY AN OLD LAWNMOWER. THE SHOCK TOWER WAS A BUG ZAPPER...
"AND THE DRAGON'S TEETH? JUST A STUPID RAKE LEFT IN THE GRASS."
WAIT... I HAVE THIS! THE KEY TO THE CITY!
THE MAYOR GAVE IT TO ME! IF WE FIND THE MAYOR, HE'LL TELL US THAT I REALLY JUMPED THE RAKE, AT LEAST!
YOU DID COLLIDE WITH THIS GUARDIAN OF THE GARDEN, REVEALING THE SECRET ITEM HE SO VALIANTLY PROTECTS.
DO NOT WORRY, IT IS JUST A STATUE, NOT A TOY.
WHAT AM I GOING TO DO? I CAN'T GO BACK TO REJEAN NOW...
I COULDN'T EVEN GET OUT OF THE BACKYARD...
NO. YOUR DESTINY LIES ELSEWHERE. YOU MUST LEAVE THIS PLACE.
PERHAPS NOT. BUT YOU SHOWED GREAT COURAGE AT EVERY TURN. CRASHES OR NO CRASHES, YOU BRAVED THE RAKE AND THE LAWNMOWER AND ALL THE OTHER DANGERS HERE.
TOGETHER, WE CAN ESCAPE.
DO YOU KNOW THE WAY OUT?

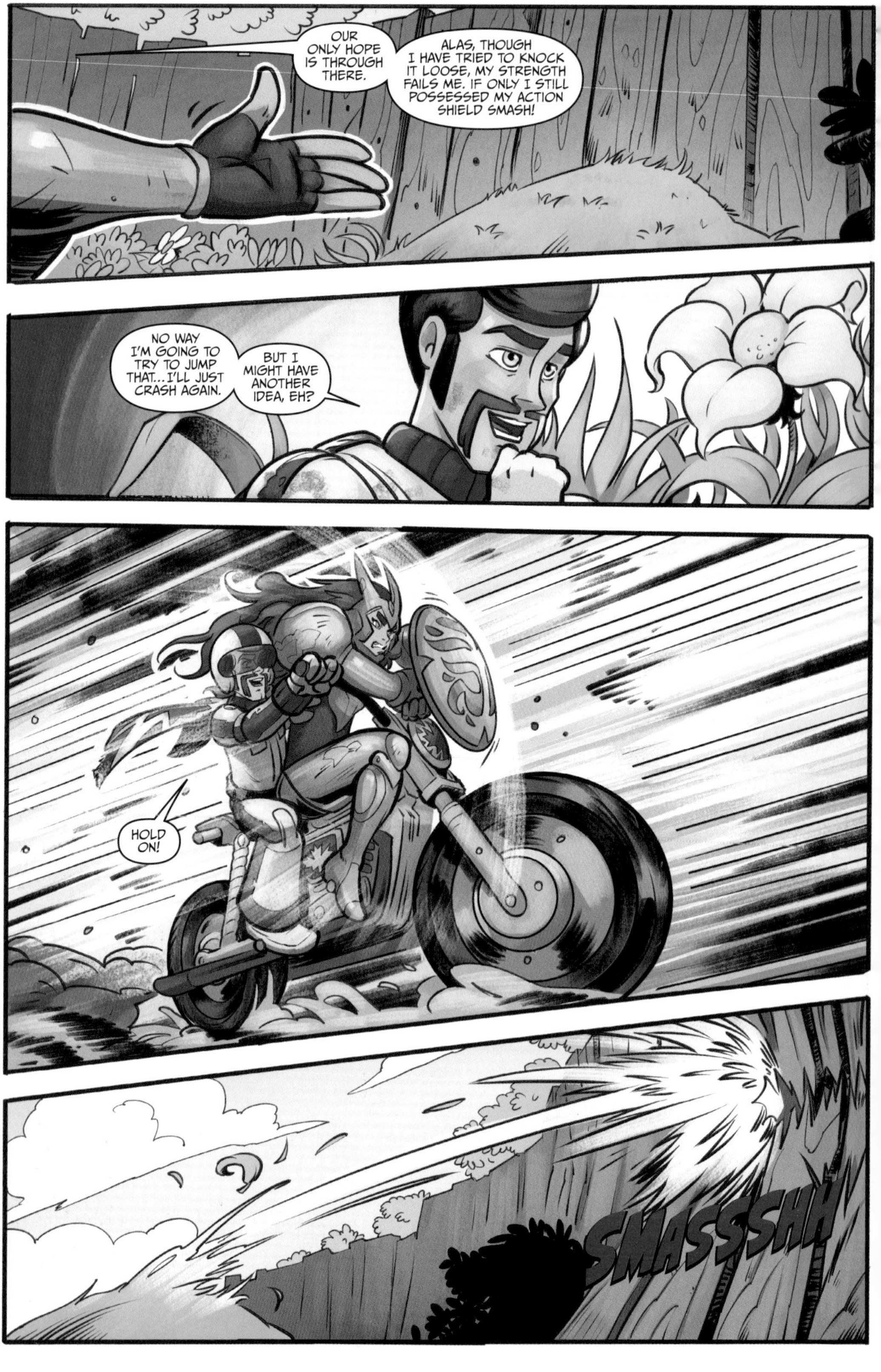
OUR ONLY HOPE IS THROUGH THERE.
ALAS, THOUGH I HAVE TRIED TO KNOCK IT LOOSE, MY STRENGTH FAILS ME. IF ONLY I STILL POSSESSED MY ACTION SHIELD SMASH!
NO WAY I'M GOING TO TRY TO JUMP THAT...I'LL JUST CRASH AGAIN.
BUT I MIGHT HAVE ANOTHER IDEA, EH?
HOLD ON!
SMASSSHH

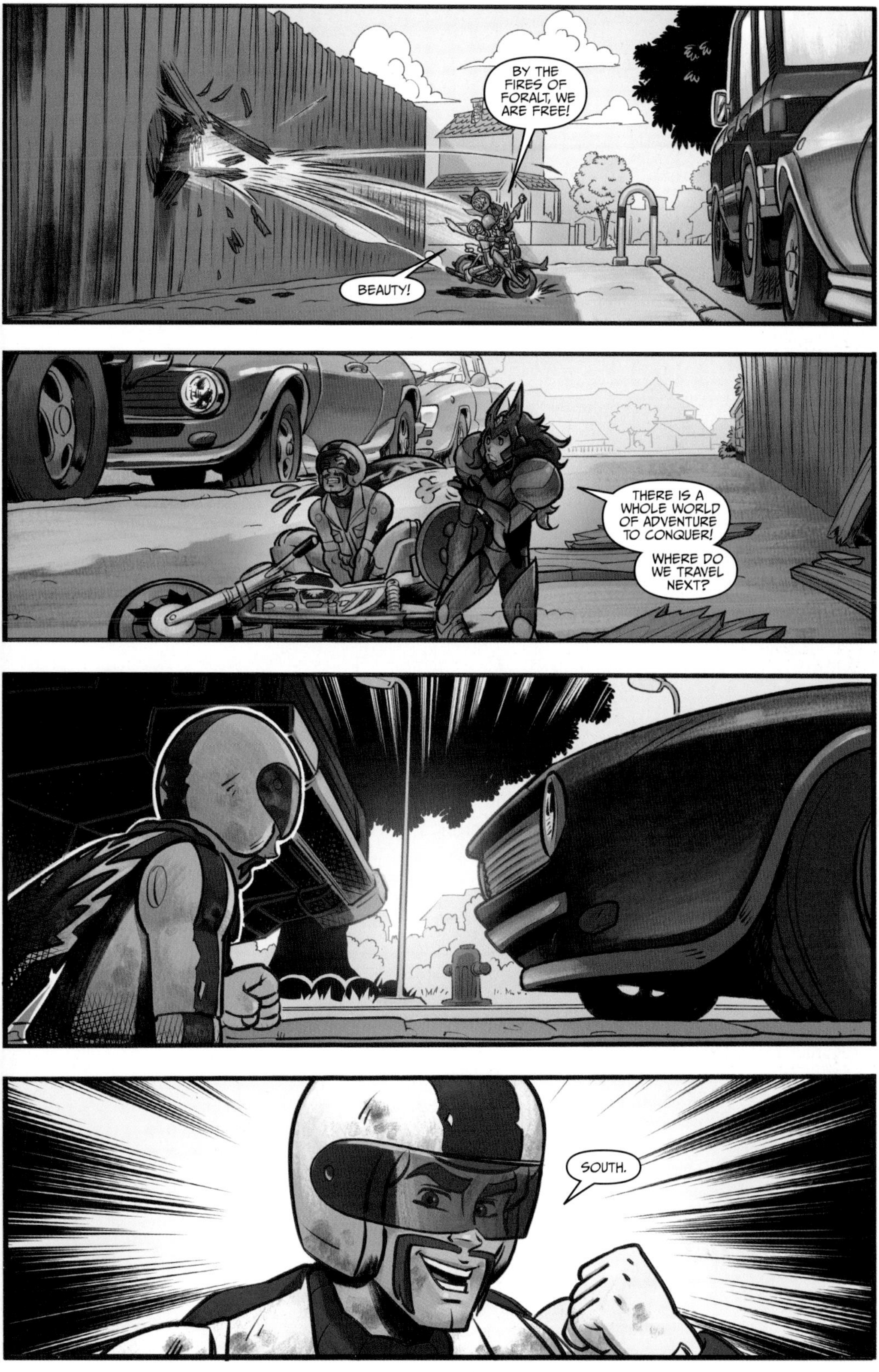
BY THE FIRES OF FORALT, WE ARE FREE!
BEAUTY!
THERE IS A WHOLE WORLD OF ADVENTURE TO CONQUER!
WHERE DO WE TRAVEL NEXT?
SOUTH.

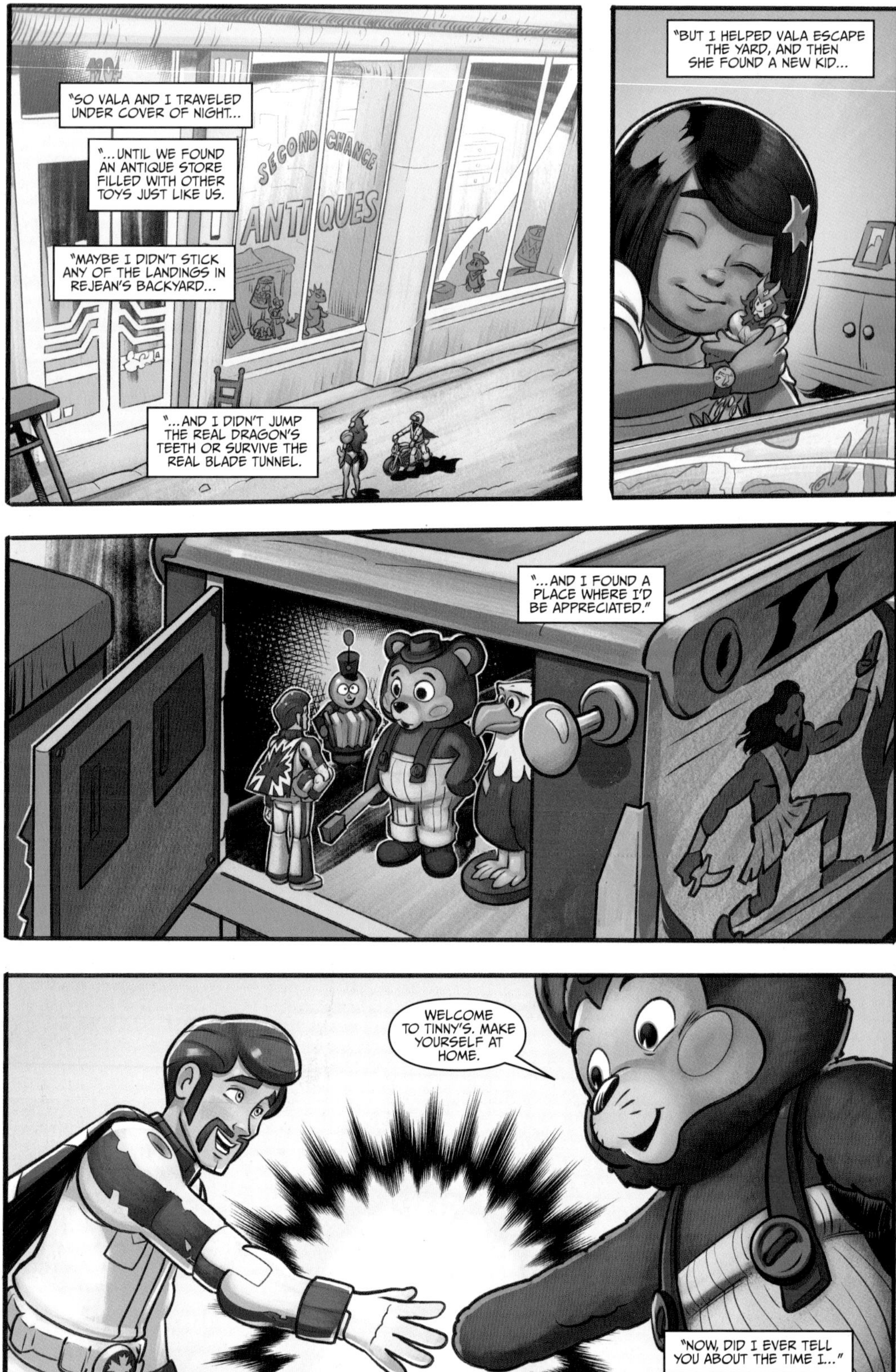

SECOND CHANCE
ANTIQUES
"SO VALA AND I TRAVELED UNDER COVER OF NIGHT...
"...UNTIL WE FOUND AN ANTIQUE STORE FILLED WITH OTHER TOYS JUST LIKE US.
"MAYBE I DIDN'T STICK ANY OF THE LANDINGS IN REJEAN'S BACKYARD...
"...AND I DIDN'T JUMP THE REAL DRAGON'S TEETH OR SURVIVE THE REAL BLADE TUNNEL.
"BUT I HELPED VALA ESCAPE THE YARD, AND THEN SHE FOUND A NEW KID...
"...AND I FOUND A PLACE WHERE I'D BE APPRECIATED."
WELCOME TO TINNY'S. MAKE YOURSELF AT HOME.
"NOW, DID I EVER TELL YOU ABOUT THE TIME I..."

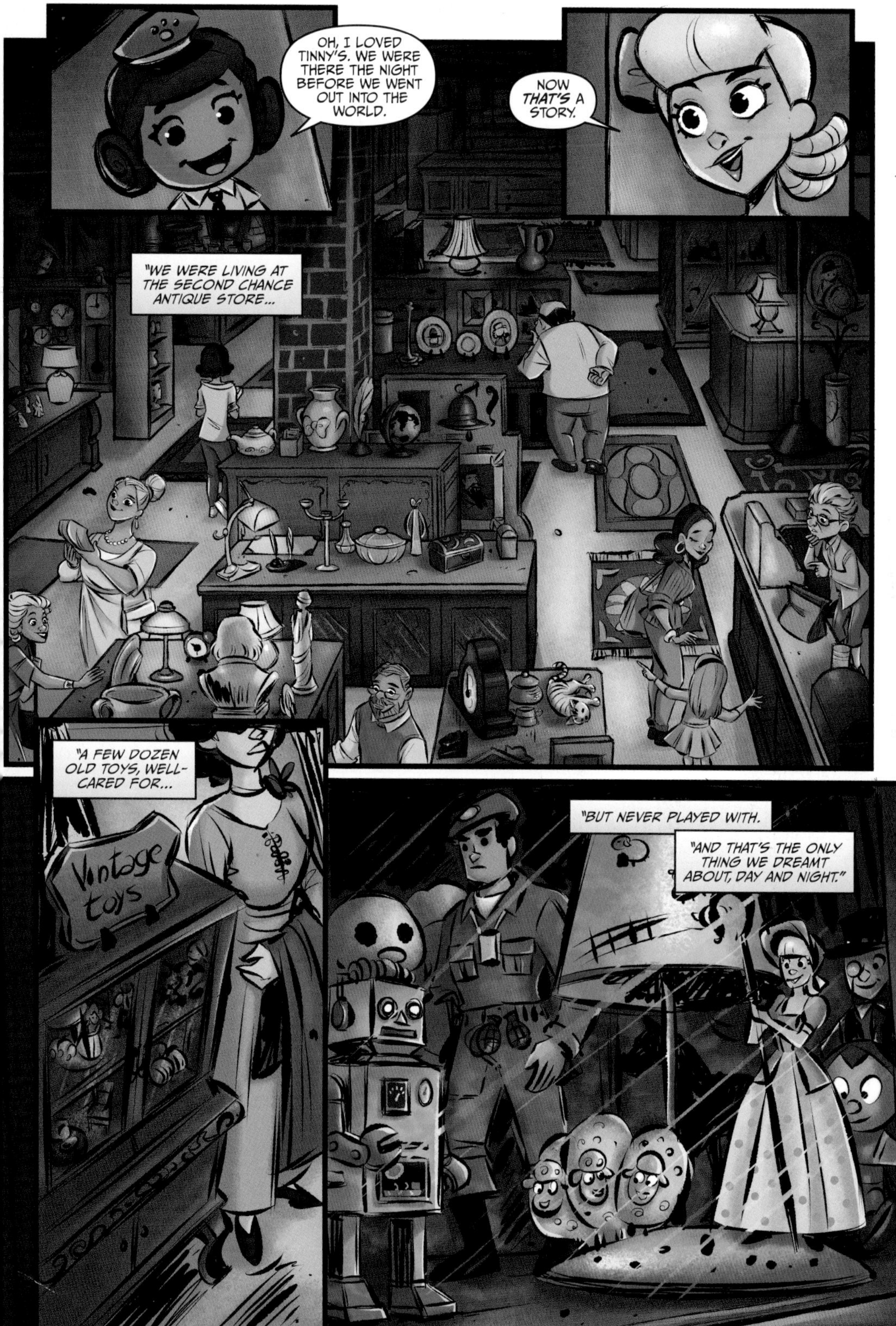
OH, I LOVED TINNY'S. WE WERE THERE THE NIGHT BEFORE WE WENT OUT INTO THE WORLD.
NOW THAT'S A STORY.
"WE WERE LIVING AT THE SECOND CHANCE ANTIQUE STORE...
"A FEW DOZEN OLD TOYS, WELL-CARED FOR...
Vintage toys
"BUT NEVER PLAYED WITH.
"AND THAT'S THE ONLY THING WE DREAMT ABOUT, DAY AND NIGHT."

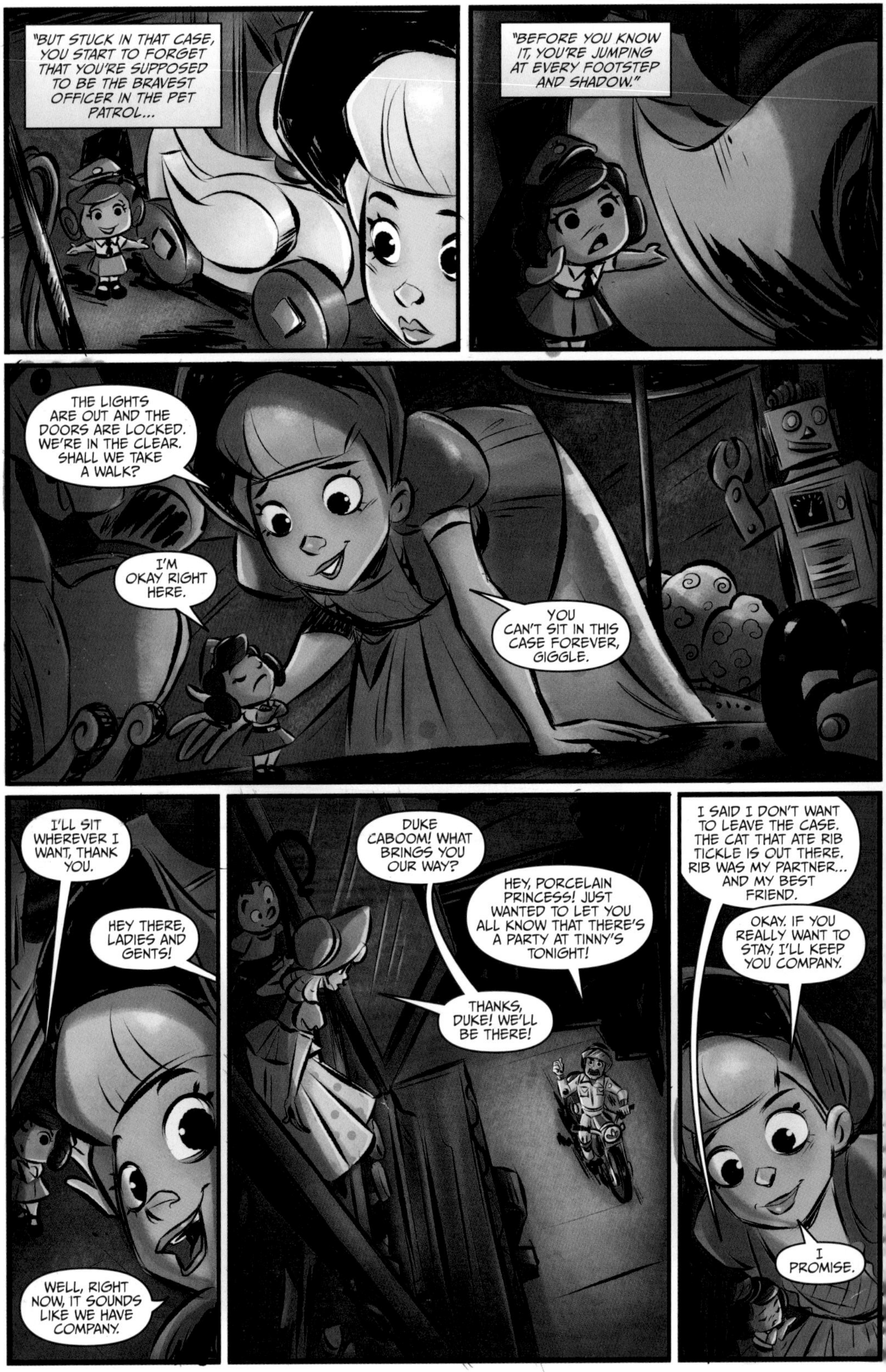
"BUT STUCK IN THAT CASE, YOU START TO FORGET THAT YOU'RE SUPPOSED TO BE THE BRAVEST OFFICER IN THE PET PATROL...
"BEFORE YOU KNOW IT, YOU'RE JUMPING AT EVERY FOOTSTEP AND SHADOW."
THE LIGHTS ARE OUT AND THE DOORS ARE LOCKED. WE'RE IN THE CLEAR. SHALL WE TAKE A WALK?
I'M OKAY RIGHT HERE.
YOU CAN'T SIT IN THIS CASE FOREVER, GIGGLE.
I'LL SIT WHEREVER I WANT, THANK YOU.
HEY THERE, LADIES AND GENTS!
WELL, RIGHT NOW, IT SOUNDS LIKE WE HAVE COMPANY.
DUKE CABOOM! WHAT BRINGS YOU OUR WAY?
HEY, PORCELAIN PRINCESS! JUST WANTED TO LET YOU ALL KNOW THAT THERE'S A PARTY AT TINNY'S TONIGHT!
THANKS, DUKE! WE'LL BE THERE!
I SAID I DON'T WANT TO LEAVE THE CASE. THE CAT THAT ATE RIB TICKLE IS OUT THERE. RIB WAS MY PARTNER... AND MY BEST FRIEND.
OKAY. IF YOU REALLY WANT TO STAY, I'LL KEEP YOU COMPANY.
I PROMISE.

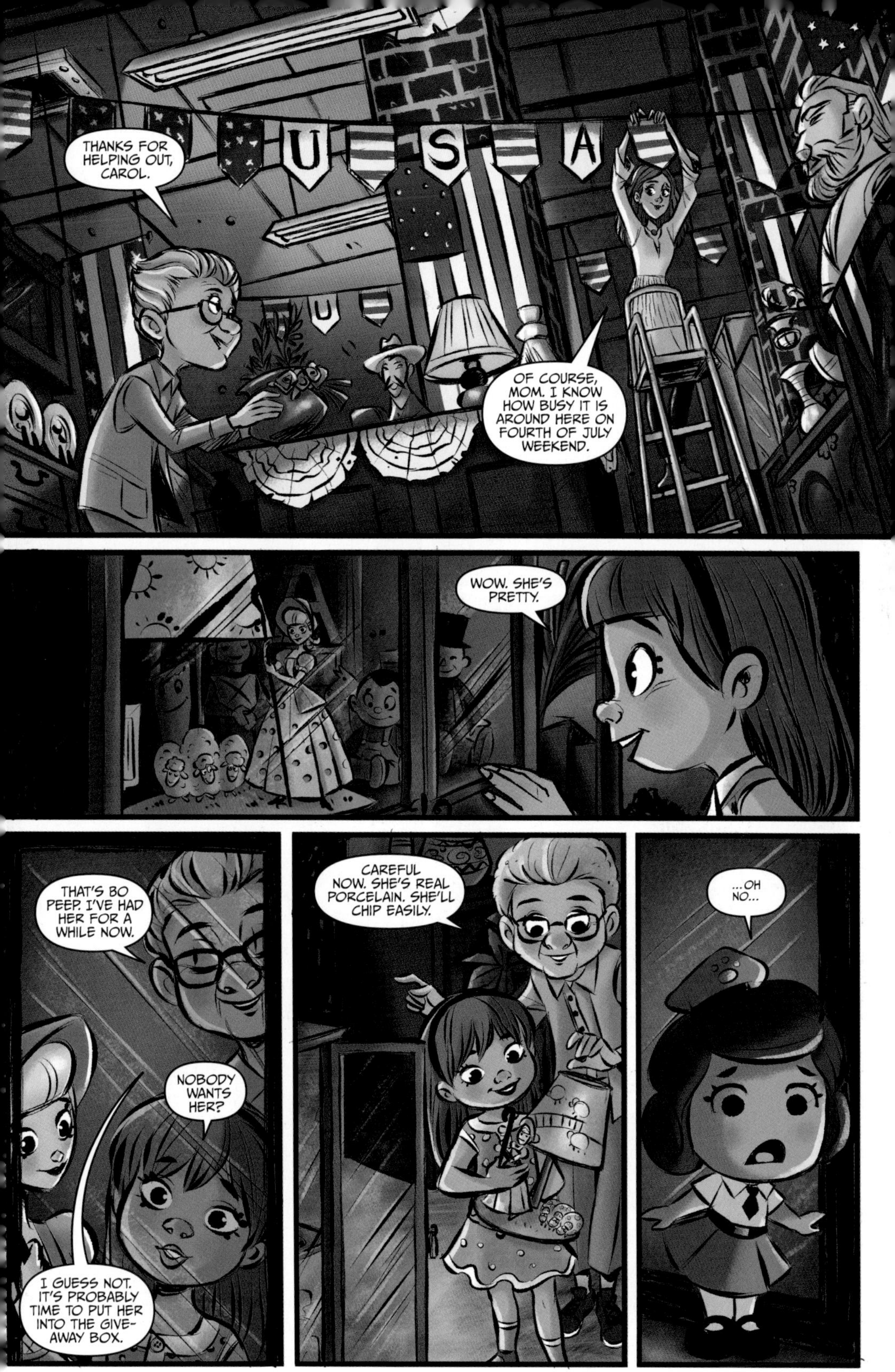
THANKS FOR HELPING OUT, CAROL.
OF COURSE, MOM. I KNOW HOW BUSY IT IS AROUND HERE ON FOURTH OF JULY WEEKEND.
U S A
WOW. SHE'S PRETTY.
THAT'S BO PEEP. I'VE HAD HER FOR A WHILE NOW.
NOBODY WANTS HER?
I GUESS NOT. IT'S PROBABLY TIME TO PUT HER INTO THE GIVE-AWAY BOX.
CAREFUL NOW. SHE'S REAL PORCELAIN. SHE'LL CHIP EASILY.
...OH NO...

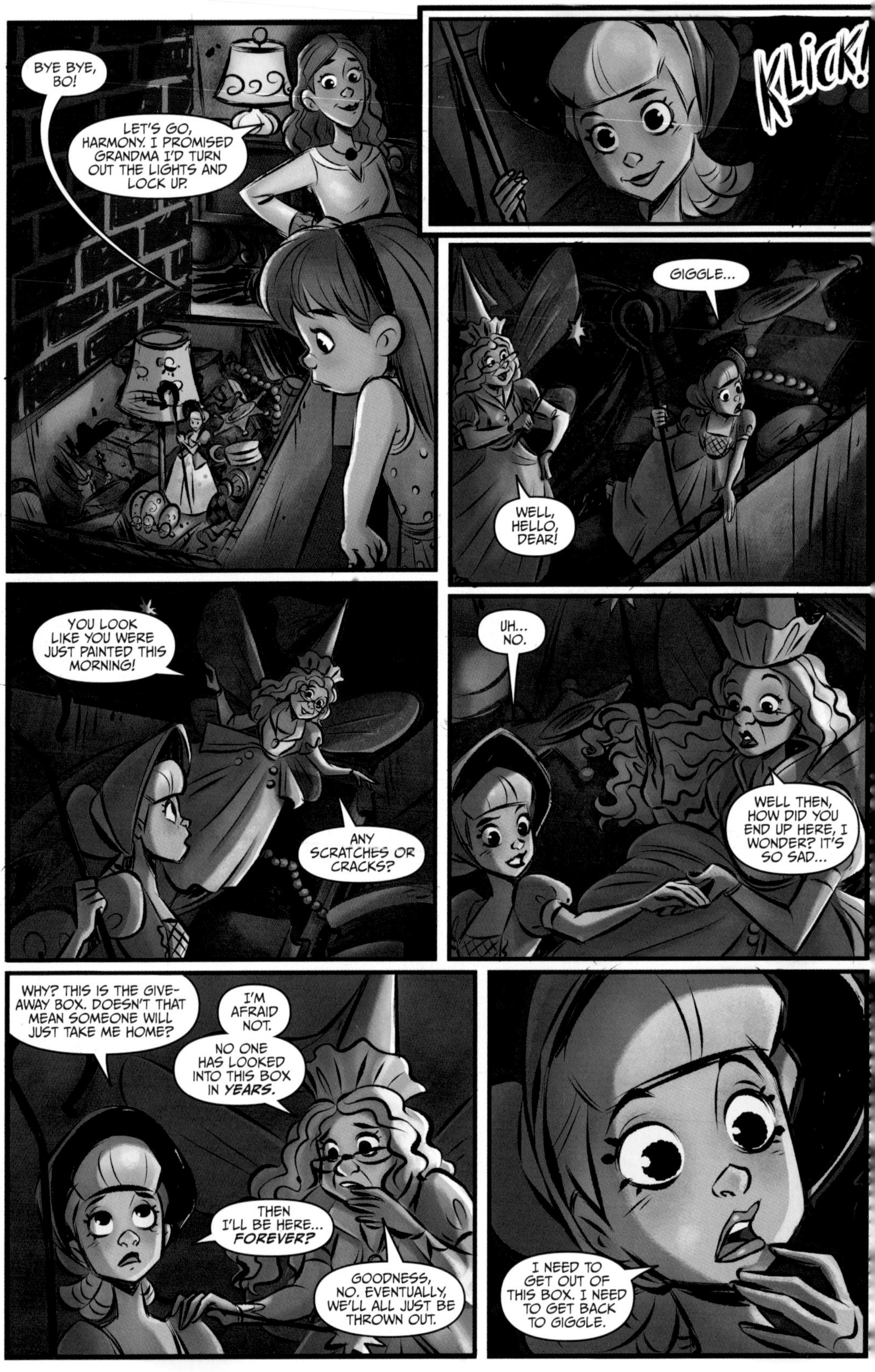
BYE BYE, BO!
LET'S GO, HARMONY. I PROMISED GRANDMA I'D TURN OUT THE LIGHTS AND LOCK UP.
KLICK!
GIGGLE...
WELL, HELLO, DEAR!
YOU LOOK LIKE YOU WERE JUST PAINTED THIS MORNING!
ANY SCRATCHES OR CRACKS?
UH... NO.
WELL THEN, HOW DID YOU END UP HERE, I WONDER? IT'S SO SAD...
WHY? THIS IS THE GIVE-AWAY BOX. DOESN'T THAT MEAN SOMEONE WILL JUST TAKE ME HOME?
I'M AFRAID NOT.
NO ONE HAS LOOKED INTO THIS BOX IN YEARS.
THEN I'LL BE HERE... FOREVER?
GOODNESS, NO. EVENTUALLY, WE'LL ALL JUST BE THROWN OUT.
I NEED TO GET OUT OF THIS BOX. I NEED TO GET BACK TO GIGGLE.

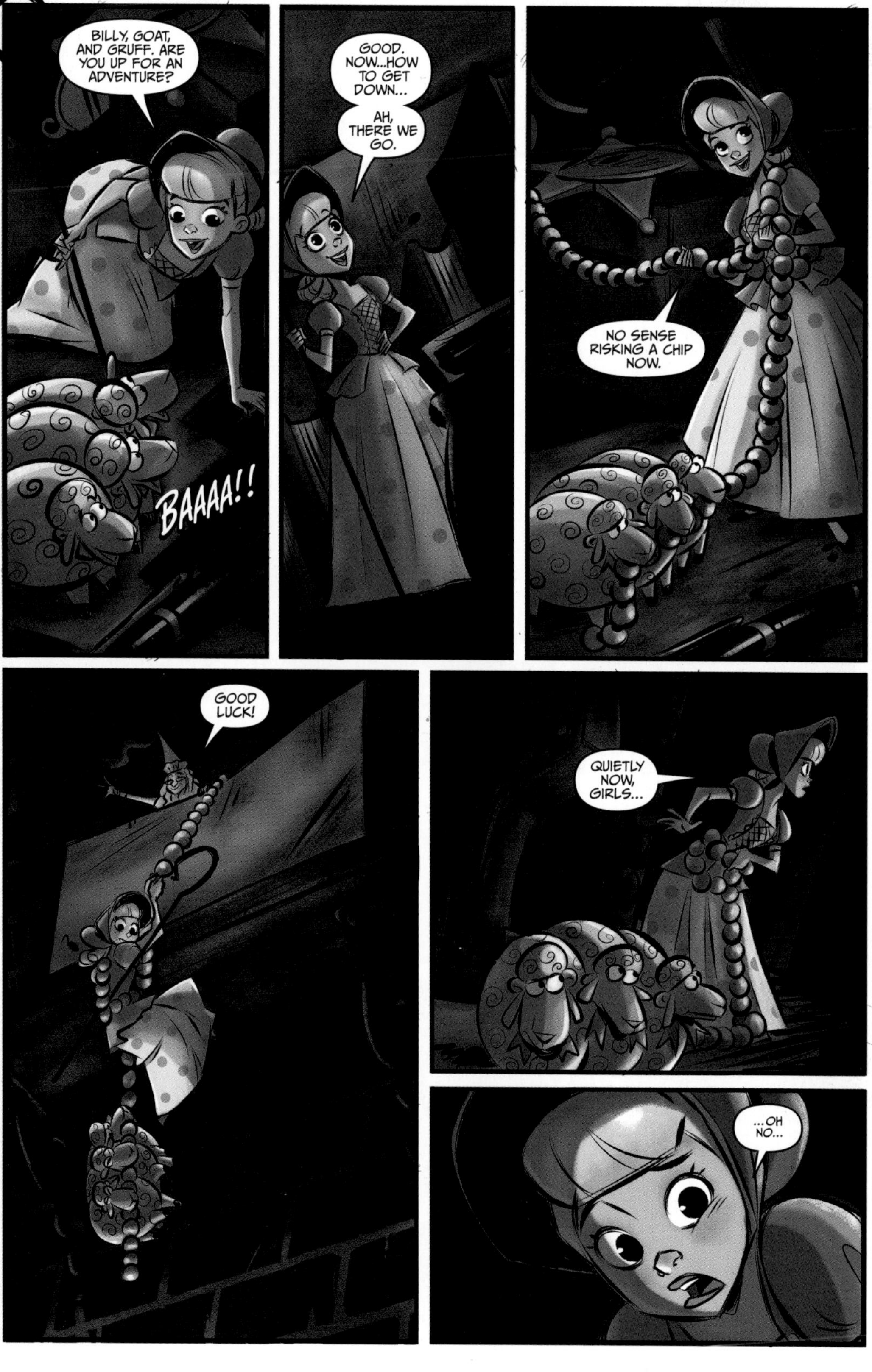
BILLY, GOAT, AND GRUFF. ARE YOU UP FOR AN ADVENTURE?
BAAAA!!
GOOD. NOW...HOW TO GET DOWN...
AH, THERE WE GO.
NO SENSE RISKING A CHIP NOW.
GOOD LUCK!
QUIETLY NOW, GIRLS...
...OH NO...

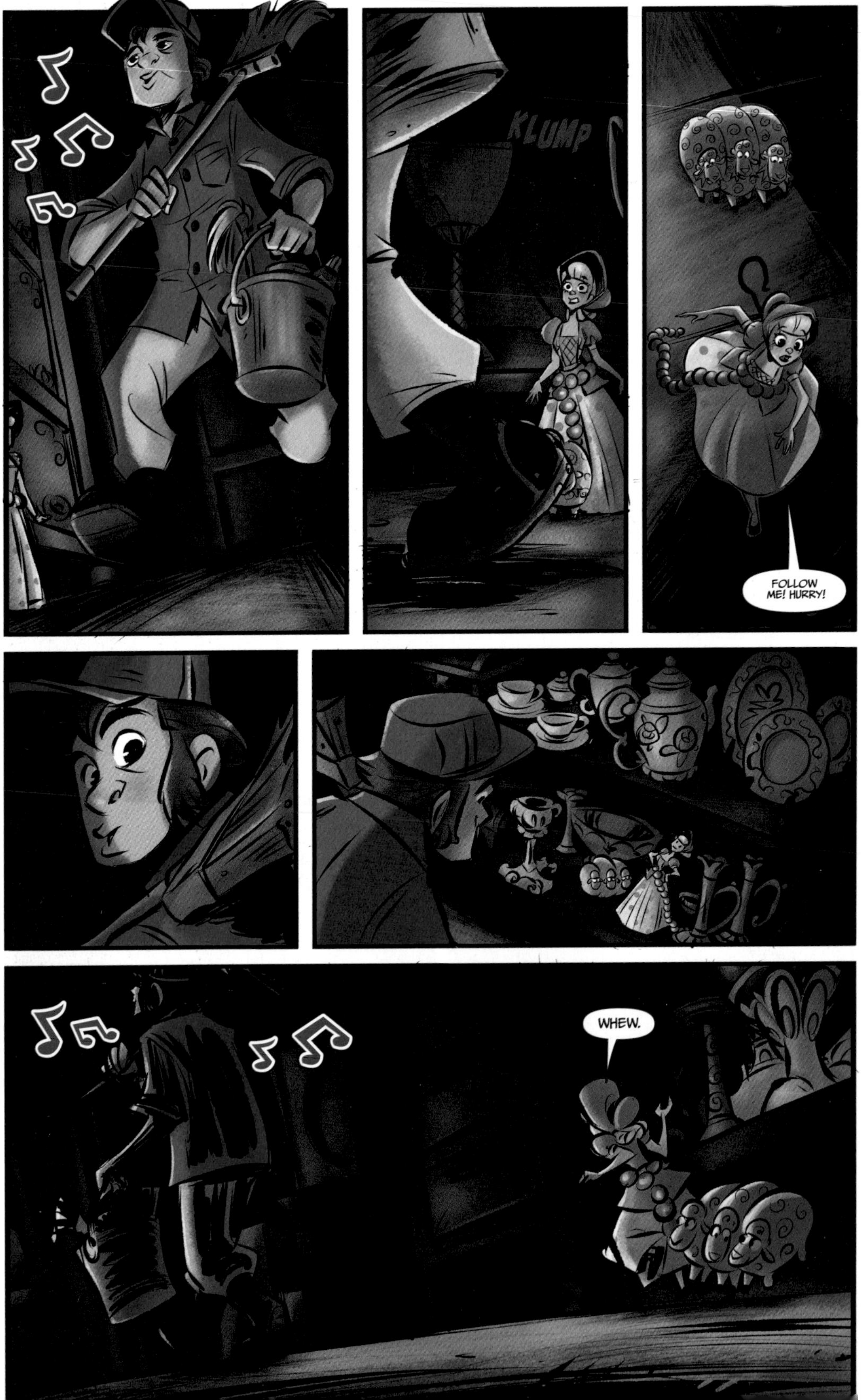
KLUMP
FOLLOW ME! HURRY!
WHEW.

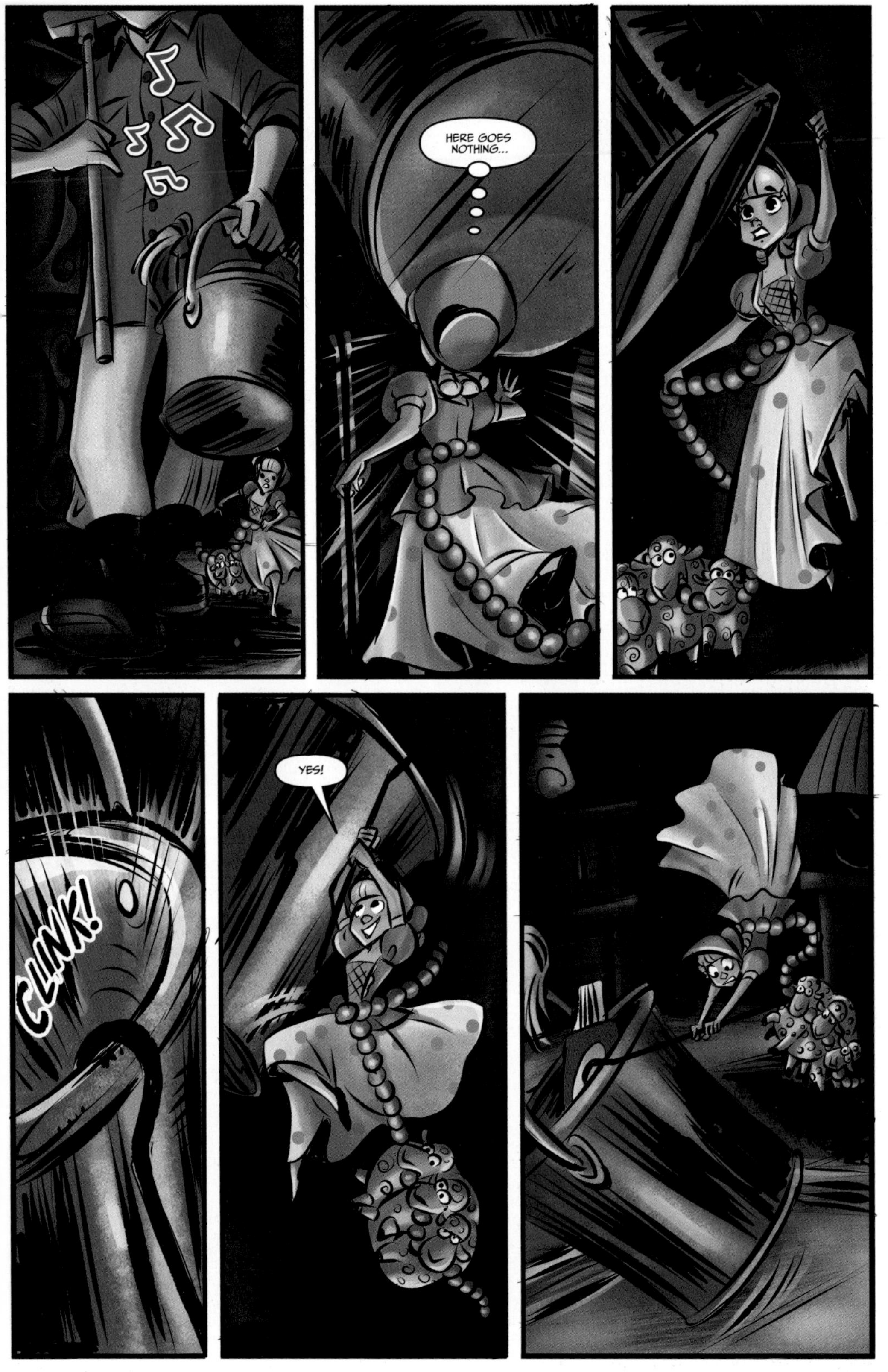
HERE GOES NOTHING...
CLINK!
YES!

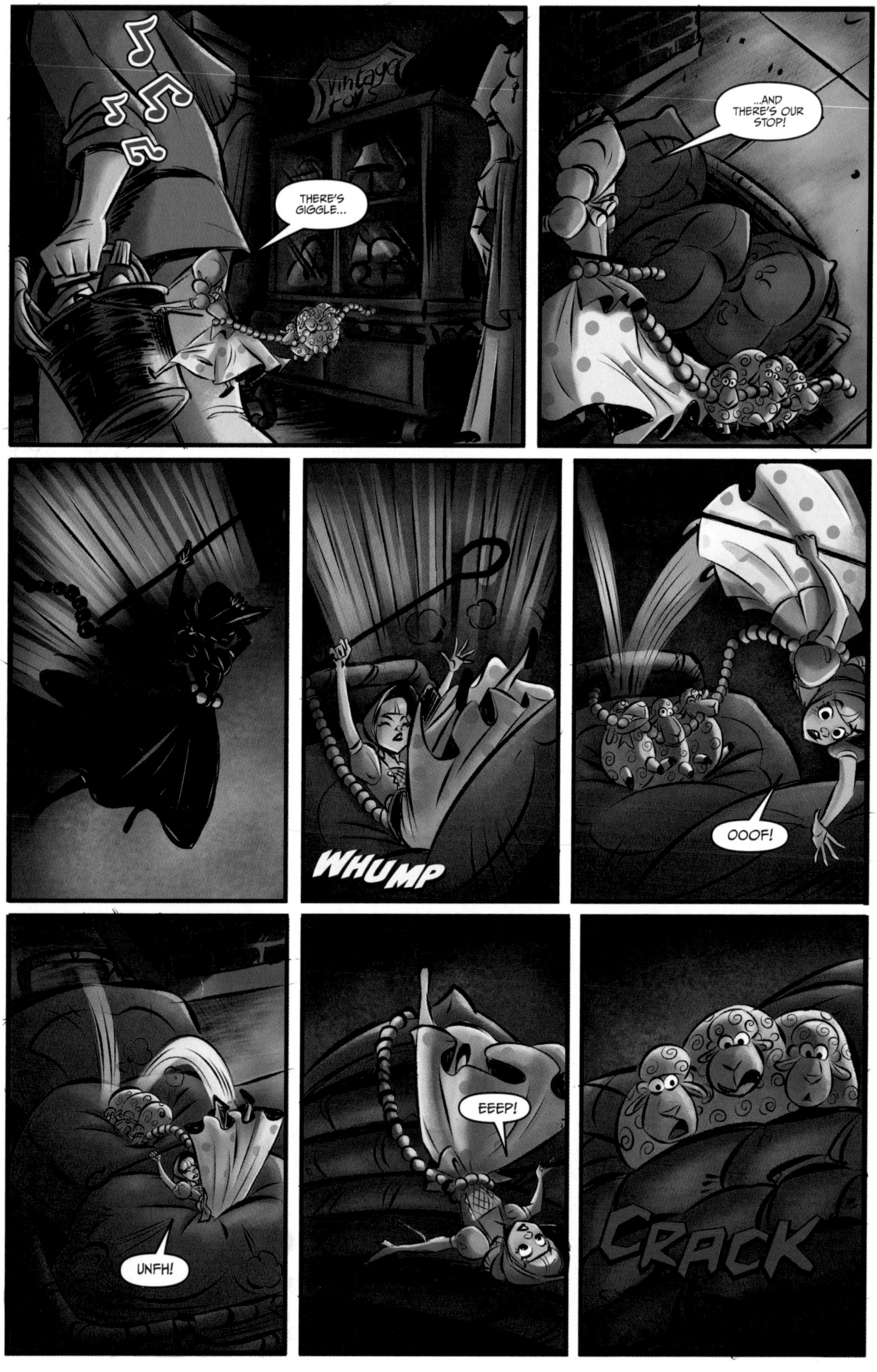
THERE'S GIGGLE...
...AND THERE'S OUR STOP!
WHUMP
OOOF!
UNFH!
EEEP!
CRACK

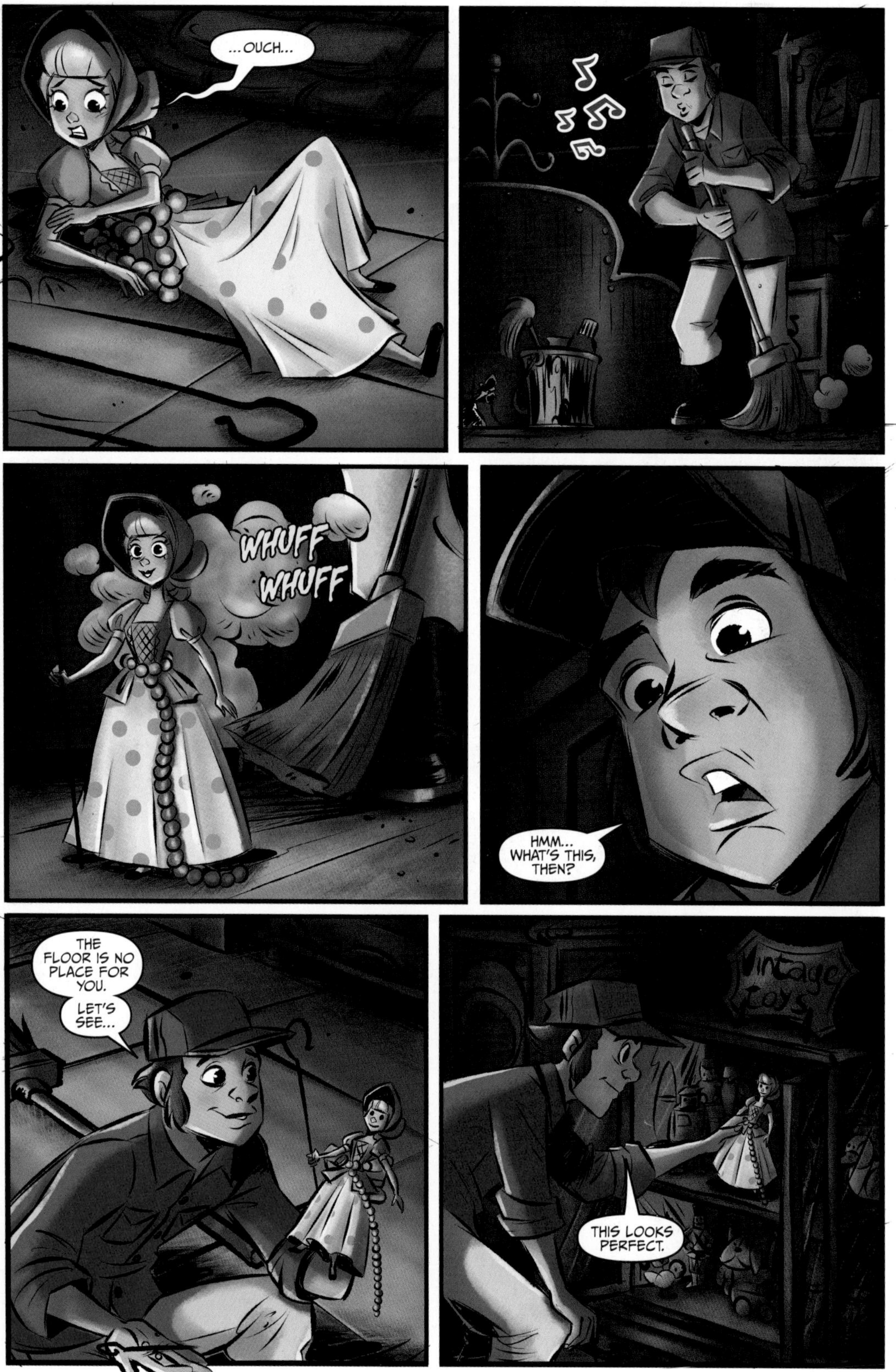
...OUCH...
WHUFF WHUFF
HMM... WHAT'S THIS, THEN?
THE FLOOR IS NO PLACE FOR YOU.
LET'S SEE...
Vintage Toys
THIS LOOKS PERFECT.

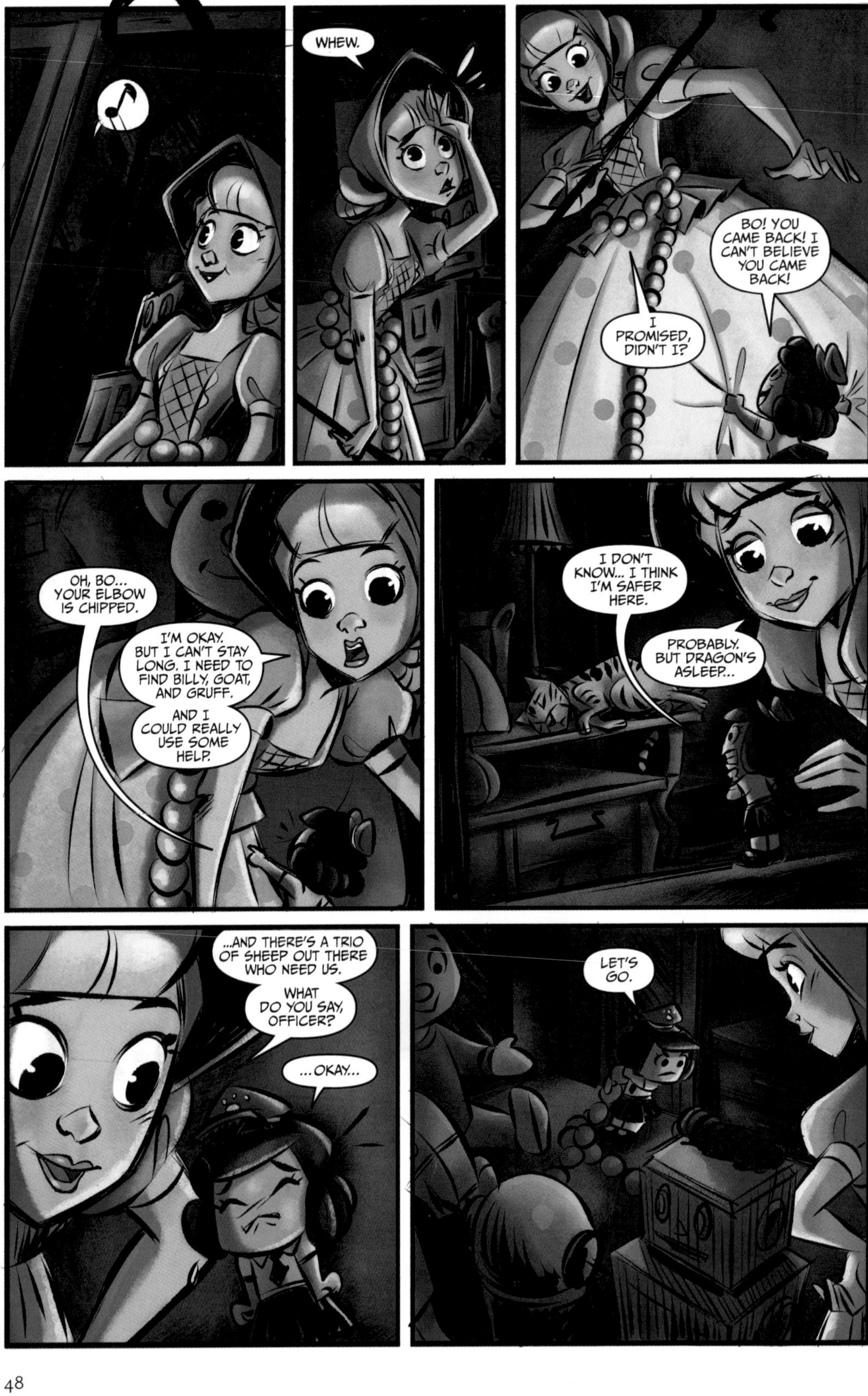
WHEW.
BO! YOU CAME BACK! I CAN'T BELIEVE YOU CAME BACK!
I PROMISED, DIDN'T I?
OH, BO... YOUR ELBOW IS CHIPPED.
I'M OKAY. BUT I CAN'T STAY LONG. I NEED TO FIND BILLY, GOAT, AND GRUFF.
AND I COULD REALLY USE SOME HELP.
I DON'T KNOW... I THINK I'M SAFER HERE.
PROBABLY. BUT DRAGON'S ASLEEP...
...AND THERE'S A TRIO OF SHEEP OUT THERE WHO NEED US.
WHAT DO YOU SAY, OFFICER?
...OKAY...
LET'S GO.

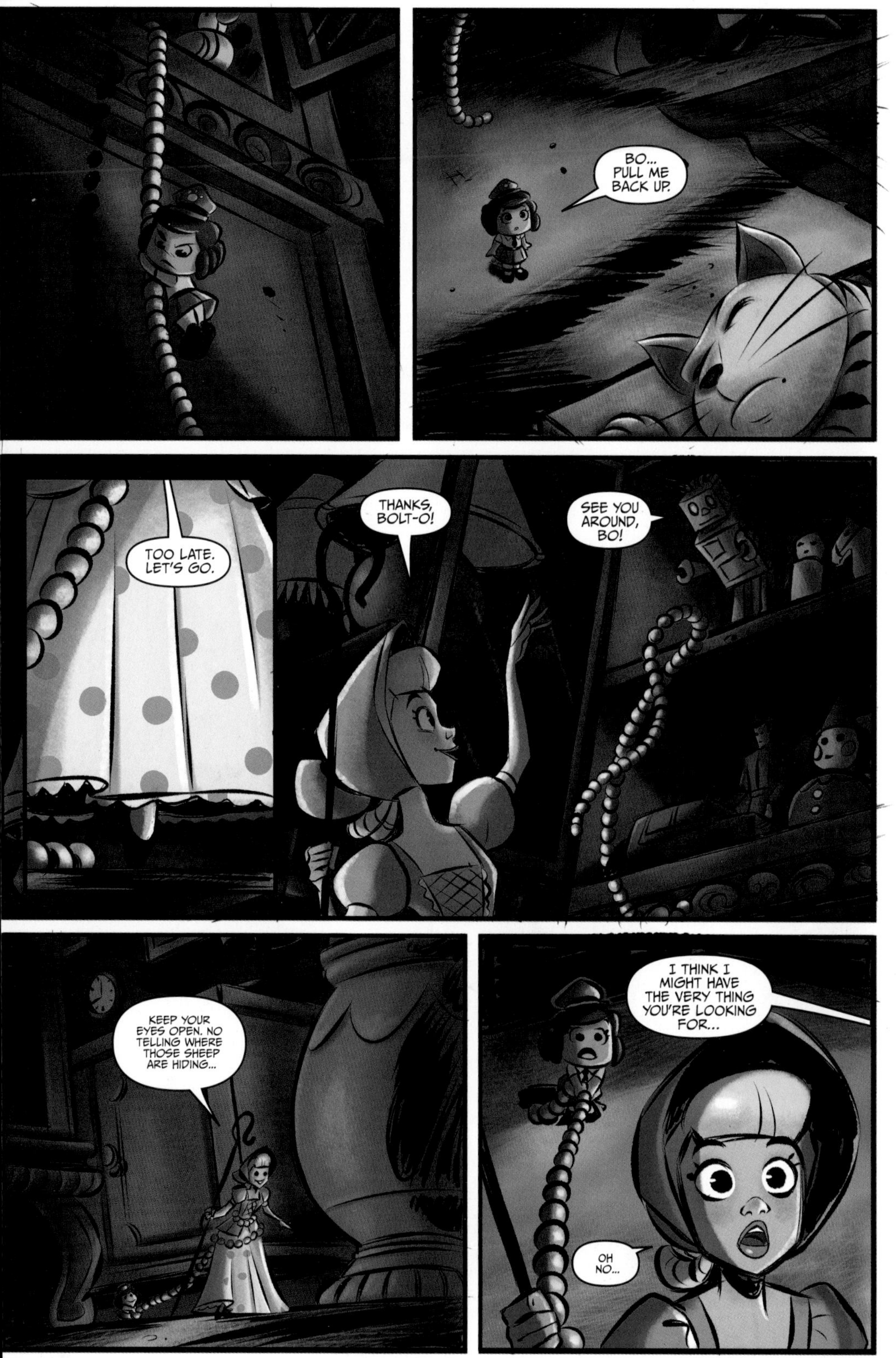
BO... PULL ME BACK UP.
TOO LATE. LET'S GO.
THANKS, BOLT-O!
SEE YOU AROUND, BO!
KEEP YOUR EYES OPEN. NO TELLING WHERE THOSE SHEEP ARE HIDING...
I THINK I MIGHT HAVE THE VERY THING YOU'RE LOOKING FOR...
OH NO...

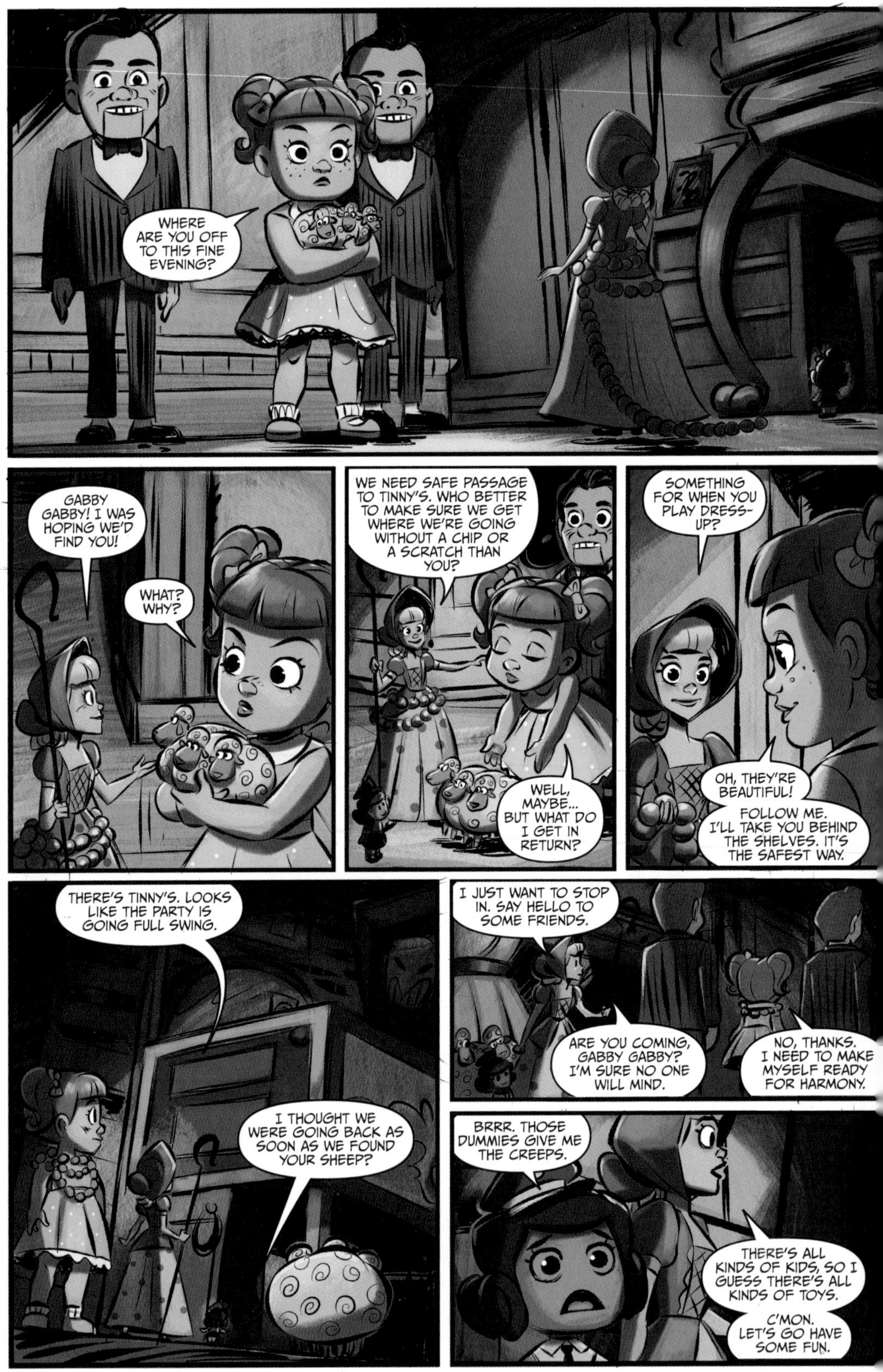
WHERE ARE YOU OFF TO THIS FINE EVENING?
GABBY GABBY! I WAS HOPING WE'D FIND YOU!
WHAT? WHY?
WE NEED SAFE PASSAGE TO TINNY'S. WHO BETTER TO MAKE SURE WE GET WHERE WE'RE GOING WITHOUT A CHIP OR A SCRATCH THAN YOU?
WELL, MAYBE... BUT WHAT DO I GET IN RETURN?
SOMETHING FOR WHEN YOU PLAY DRESS-UP?
OH, THEY'RE BEAUTIFUL!
FOLLOW ME. I'LL TAKE YOU BEHIND THE SHELVES. IT'S THE SAFEST WAY.
THERE'S TINNY'S. LOOKS LIKE THE PARTY IS GOING FULL SWING.
I THOUGHT WE WERE GOING BACK AS SOON AS WE FOUND YOUR SHEEP?
I JUST WANT TO STOP IN. SAY HELLO TO SOME FRIENDS.
ARE YOU COMING, GABBY GABBY? I'M SURE NO ONE WILL MIND.
NO, THANKS. I NEED TO MAKE MYSELF READY FOR HARMONY.
BRRR. THOSE DUMMIES GIVE ME THE CREEPS.
THERE'S ALL KINDS OF KIDS, SO I GUESS THERE'S ALL KINDS OF TOYS.
C'MON. LET'S GO HAVE SOME FUN.

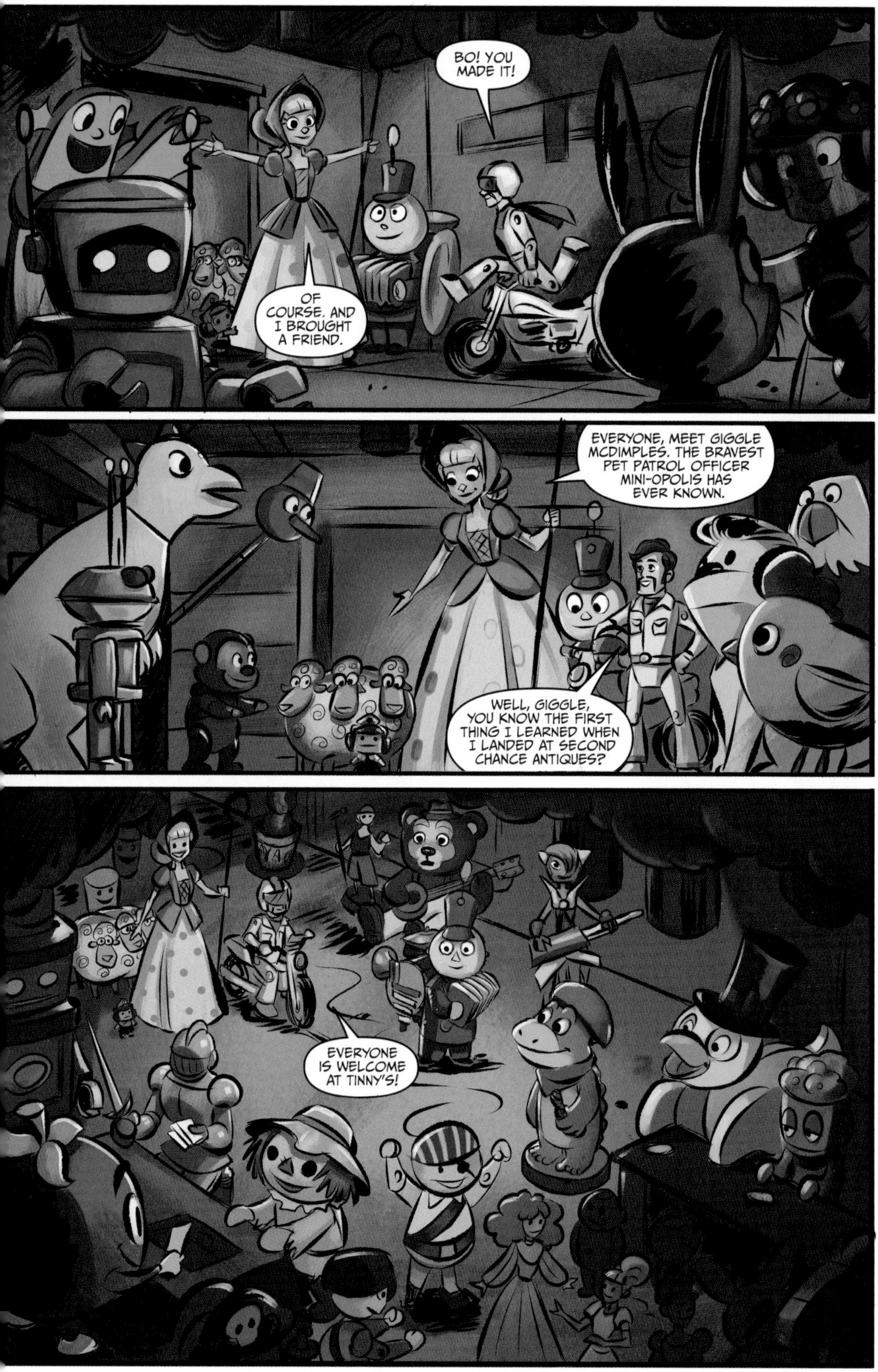
BO! YOU MADE IT!
OF COURSE. AND I BROUGHT A FRIEND.
EVERYONE, MEET GIGGLE MCDIMPLES. THE BRAVEST PET PATROL OFFICER MINI-OPOLIS HAS EVER KNOWN.
WELL, GIGGLE, YOU KNOW THE FIRST THING I LEARNED WHEN I LANDED AT SECOND CHANCE ANTIQUES?
EVERYONE IS WELCOME AT TINNY'S!

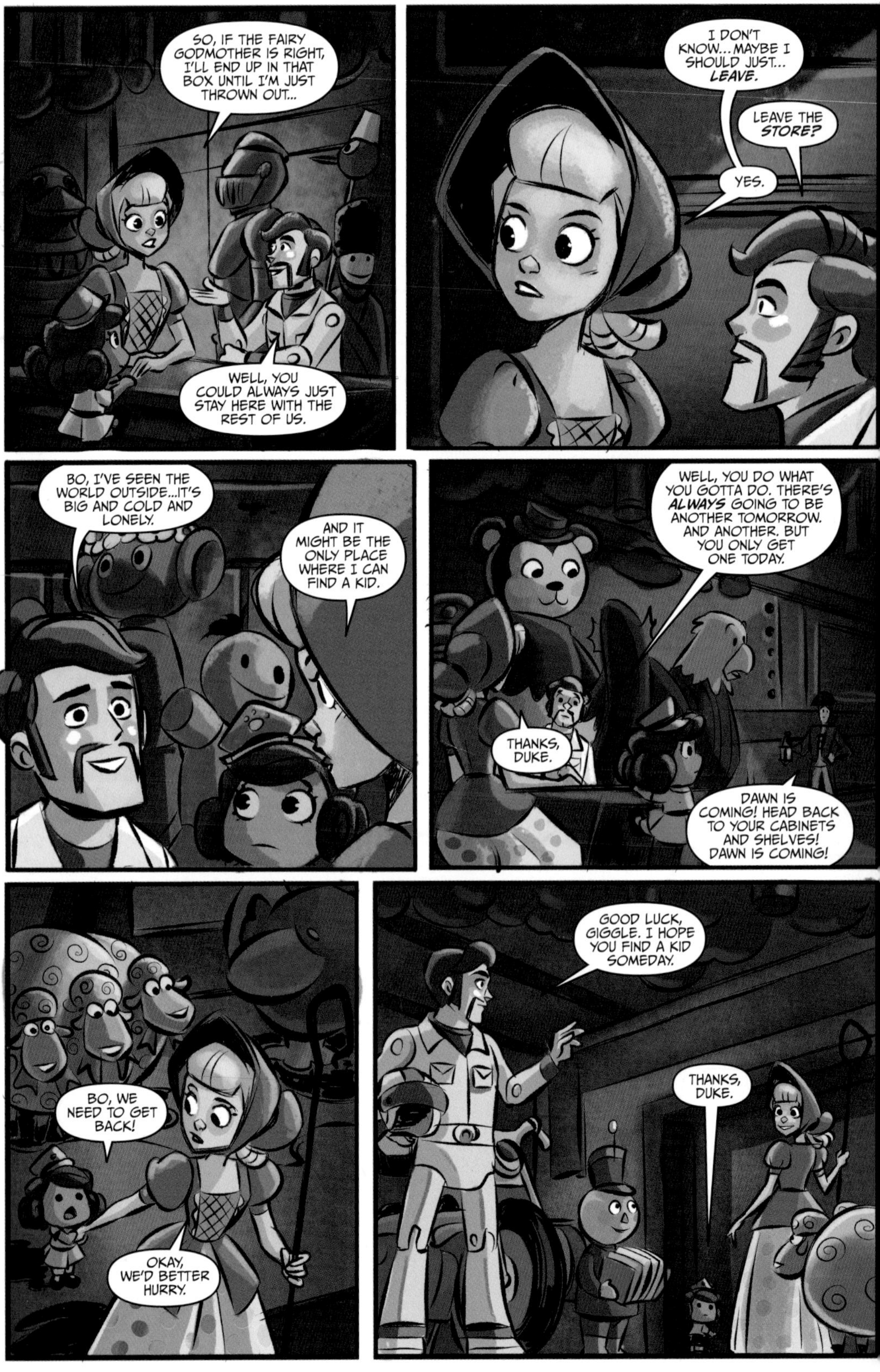
SO, IF THE FAIRY GODMOTHER IS RIGHT, I'LL END UP IN THAT BOX UNTIL I'M JUST THROWN OUT...
WELL, YOU COULD ALWAYS JUST STAY HERE WITH THE REST OF US.
I DON'T KNOW... MAYBE I SHOULD JUST... LEAVE.
LEAVE THE STORE?
YES.
BO, I'VE SEEN THE WORLD OUTSIDE...IT'S BIG AND COLD AND LONELY.
AND IT MIGHT BE THE ONLY PLACE WHERE I CAN FIND A KID.
WELL, YOU DO WHAT YOU GOTTA DO. THERE'S ALWAYS GOING TO BE ANOTHER TOMORROW. AND ANOTHER. BUT YOU ONLY GET ONE TODAY.
THANKS, DUKE.
DAWN IS COMING! HEAD BACK TO YOUR CABINETS AND SHELVES! DAWN IS COMING!
BO, WE NEED TO GET BACK!
OKAY, WE'D BETTER HURRY.
GOOD LUCK, GIGGLE. I HOPE YOU FIND A KID SOMEDAY.
THANKS, DUKE.

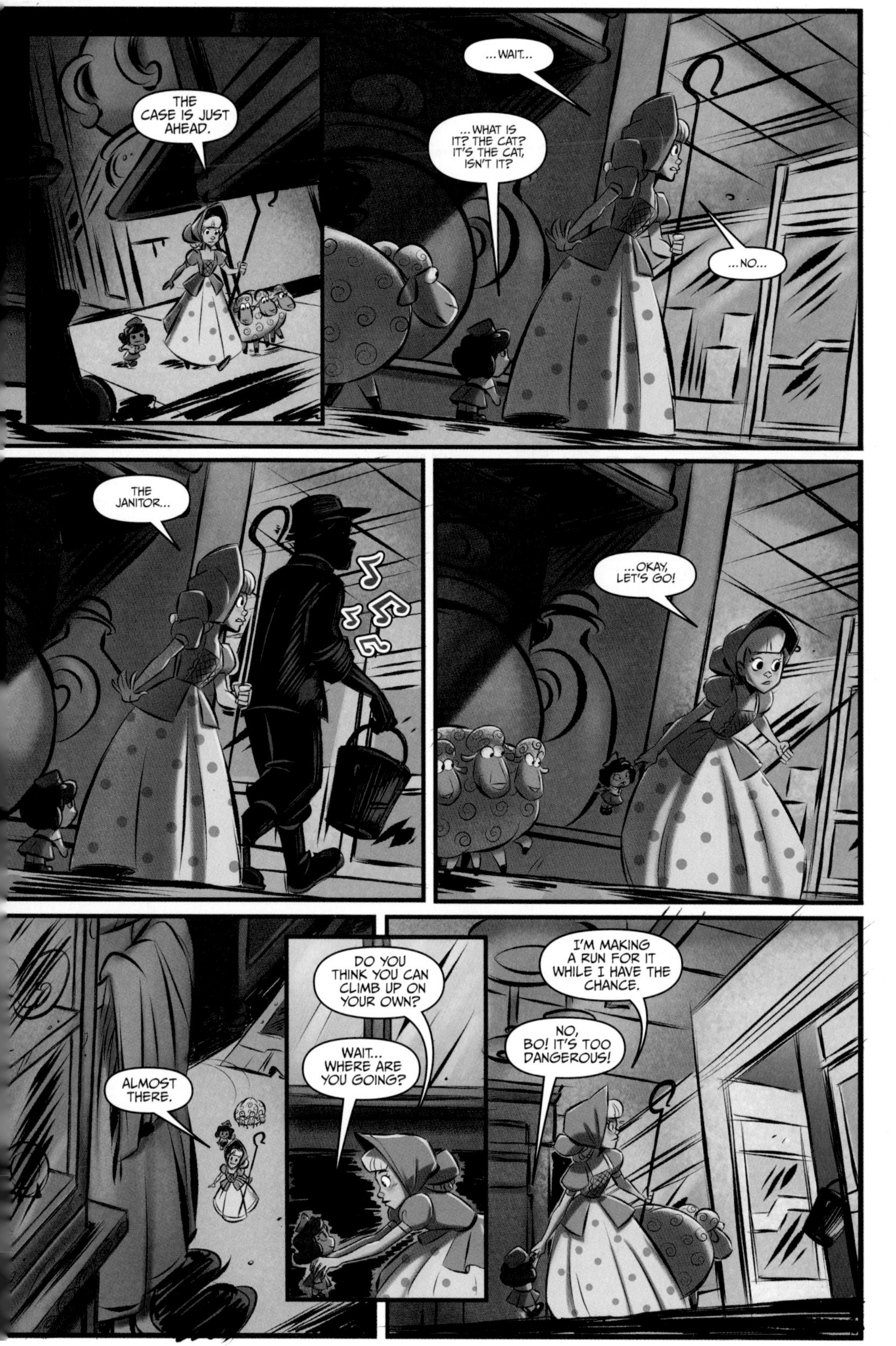
THE CASE IS JUST AHEAD.
...WAIT...
...WHAT IS IT? THE CAT? IT'S THE CAT, ISN'T IT?
...NO...
THE JANITOR...
...OKAY, LET'S GO!
ALMOST THERE.
DO YOU THINK YOU CAN CLIMB UP ON YOUR OWN?
WAIT... WHERE ARE YOU GOING?
I'M MAKING A RUN FOR IT WHILE I HAVE THE CHANCE.
NO, BO! IT'S TOO DANGEROUS!

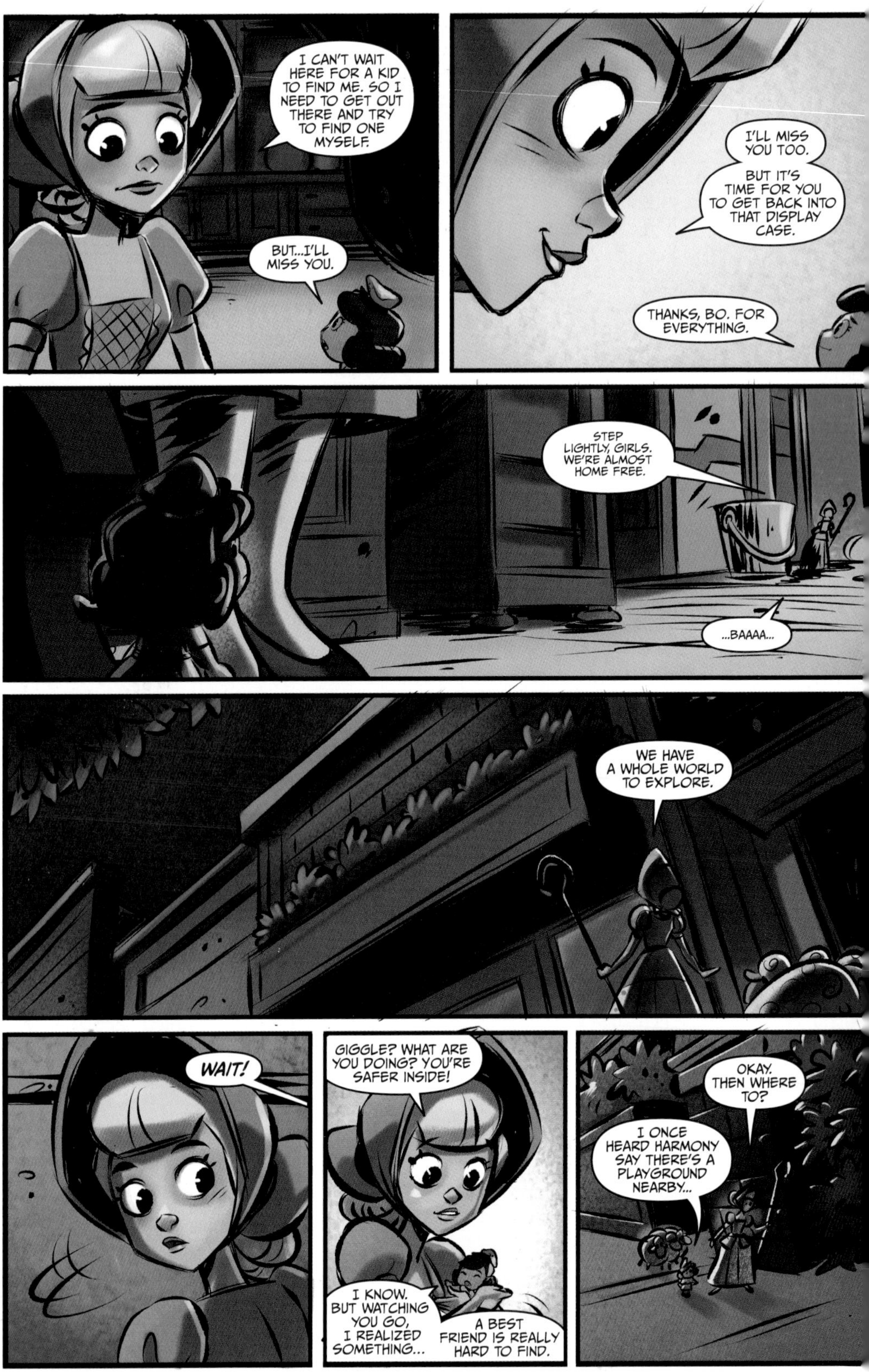
I CAN'T WAIT HERE FOR A KID TO FIND ME. SO I NEED TO GET OUT THERE AND TRY TO FIND ONE MYSELF.
BUT...I'LL MISS YOU.
I'LL MISS YOU TOO.
BUT IT'S TIME FOR YOU TO GET BACK INTO THAT DISPLAY CASE.
THANKS, BO. FOR EVERYTHING.
STEP LIGHTLY, GIRLS. WE'RE ALMOST HOME FREE.
...BAAAA...
WE HAVE A WHOLE WORLD TO EXPLORE.
WAIT!
GIGGLE? WHAT ARE YOU DOING? YOU'RE SAFER INSIDE!
I KNOW. BUT WATCHING YOU GO, I REALIZED SOMETHING...
A BEST FRIEND IS REALLY HARD TO FIND.
OKAY. THEN WHERE TO?
I ONCE HEARD HARMONY SAY THERE'S A PLAYGROUND NEARBY...

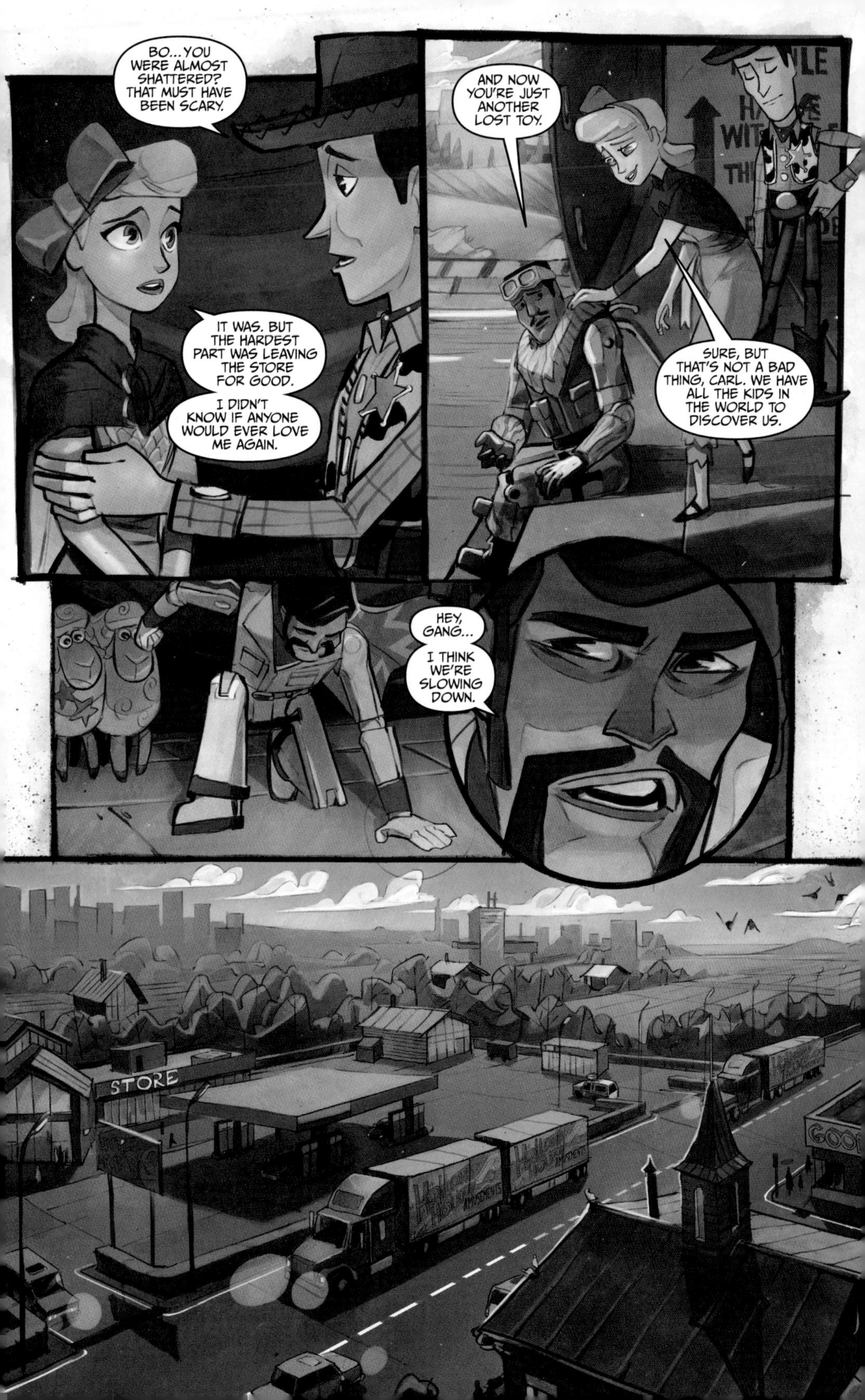
BO... YOU WERE ALMOST SHATTERED? THAT MUST HAVE BEEN SCARY.
IT WAS. BUT THE HARDEST PART WAS LEAVING THE STORE FOR GOOD.
I DIDN'T KNOW IF ANYONE WOULD EVER LOVE ME AGAIN.
AND NOW YOU'RE JUST ANOTHER LOST TOY.
SURE, BUT THAT'S NOT A BAD THING, CARL. WE HAVE ALL THE KIDS IN THE WORLD TO DISCOVER US.
HEY, GANG...
I THINK WE'RE SLOWING DOWN.
STORE

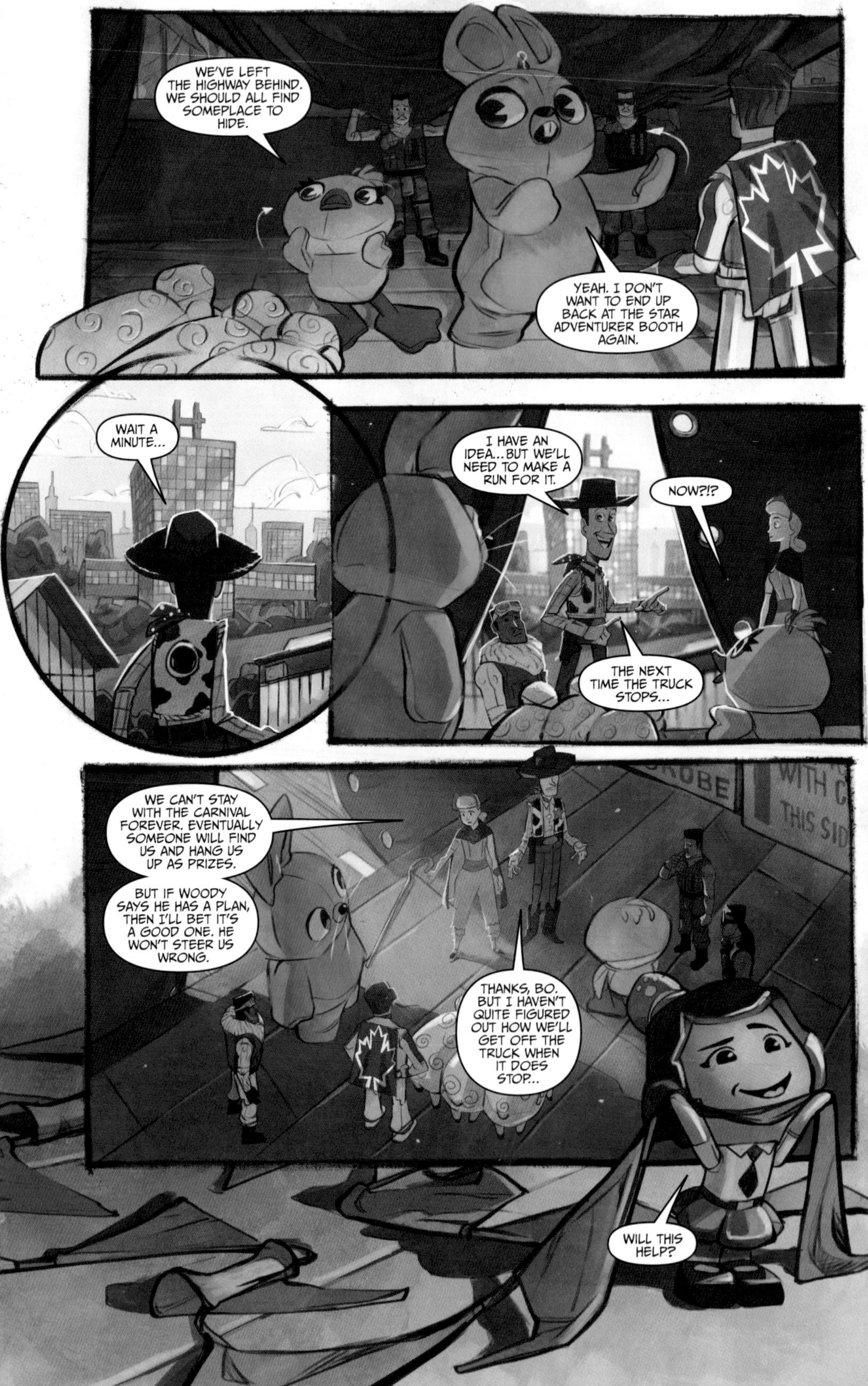
WE'VE LEFT THE HIGHWAY BEHIND. WE SHOULD ALL FIND SOMEPLACE TO HIDE.
YEAH. I DON'T WANT TO END UP BACK AT THE STAR ADVENTURER BOOTH AGAIN.
WAIT A MINUTE...
I HAVE AN IDEA...BUT WE'LL NEED TO MAKE A RUN FOR IT.
NOW?!?
THE NEXT TIME THE TRUCK STOPS...
WE CAN'T STAY WITH THE CARNIVAL FOREVER. EVENTUALLY SOMEONE WILL FIND US AND HANG US UP AS PRIZES.
BUT IF WOODY SAYS HE HAS A PLAN, THEN I'LL BET IT'S A GOOD ONE. HE WON'T STEER US WRONG.
THANKS, BO. BUT I HAVEN'T QUITE FIGURED OUT HOW WE'LL GET OFF THE TRUCK WHEN IT DOES STOP...
WILL THIS HELP?

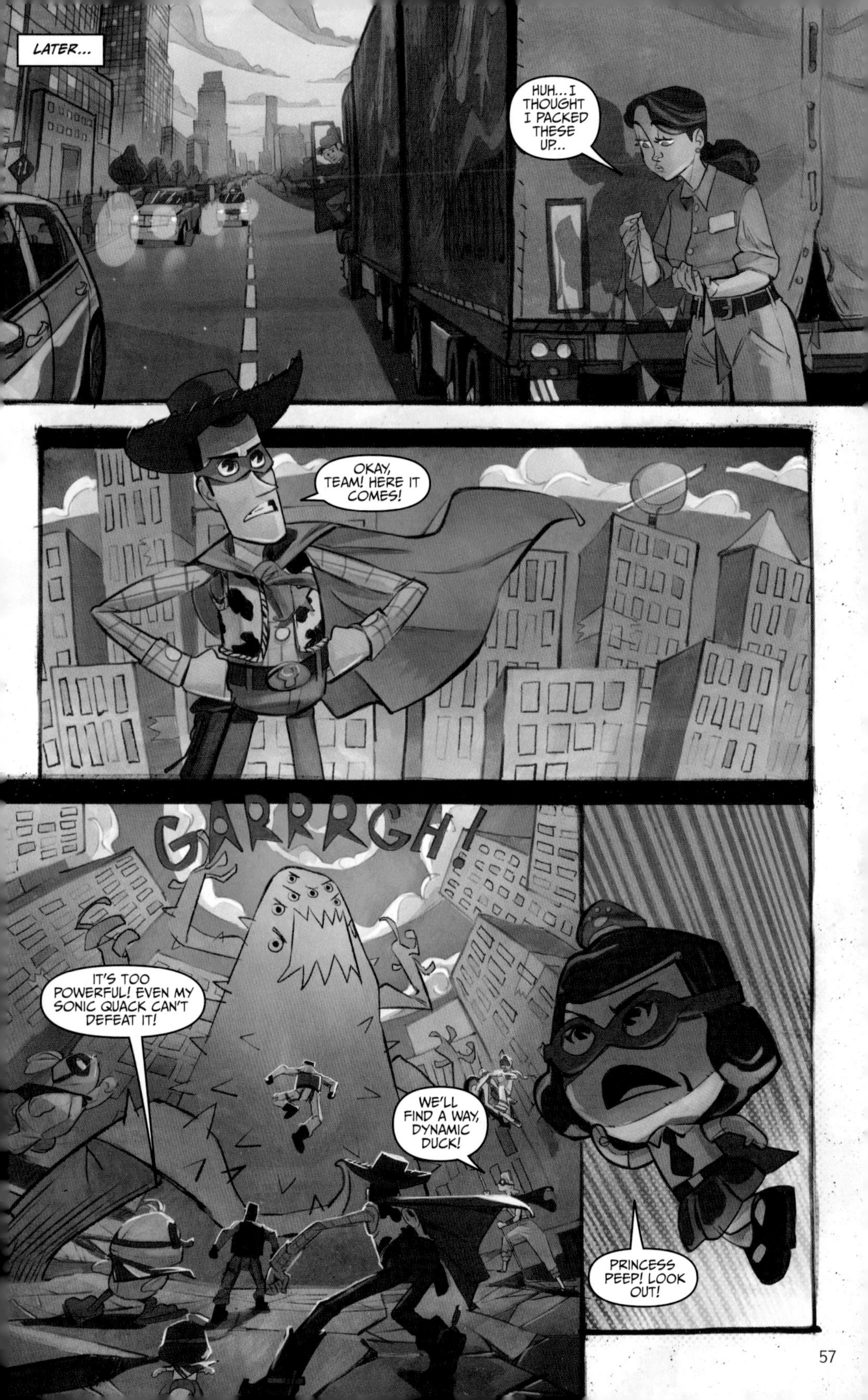
LATER...
HUH... I THOUGHT I PACKED THESE UP...
OKAY, TEAM! HERE IT COMES!
GARRRGH!
IT'S TOO POWERFUL! EVEN MY SONIC QUACK CAN'T DEFEAT IT!
WE'LL FIND A WAY, DYNAMIC DUCK!
PRINCESS PEEP! LOOK OUT!

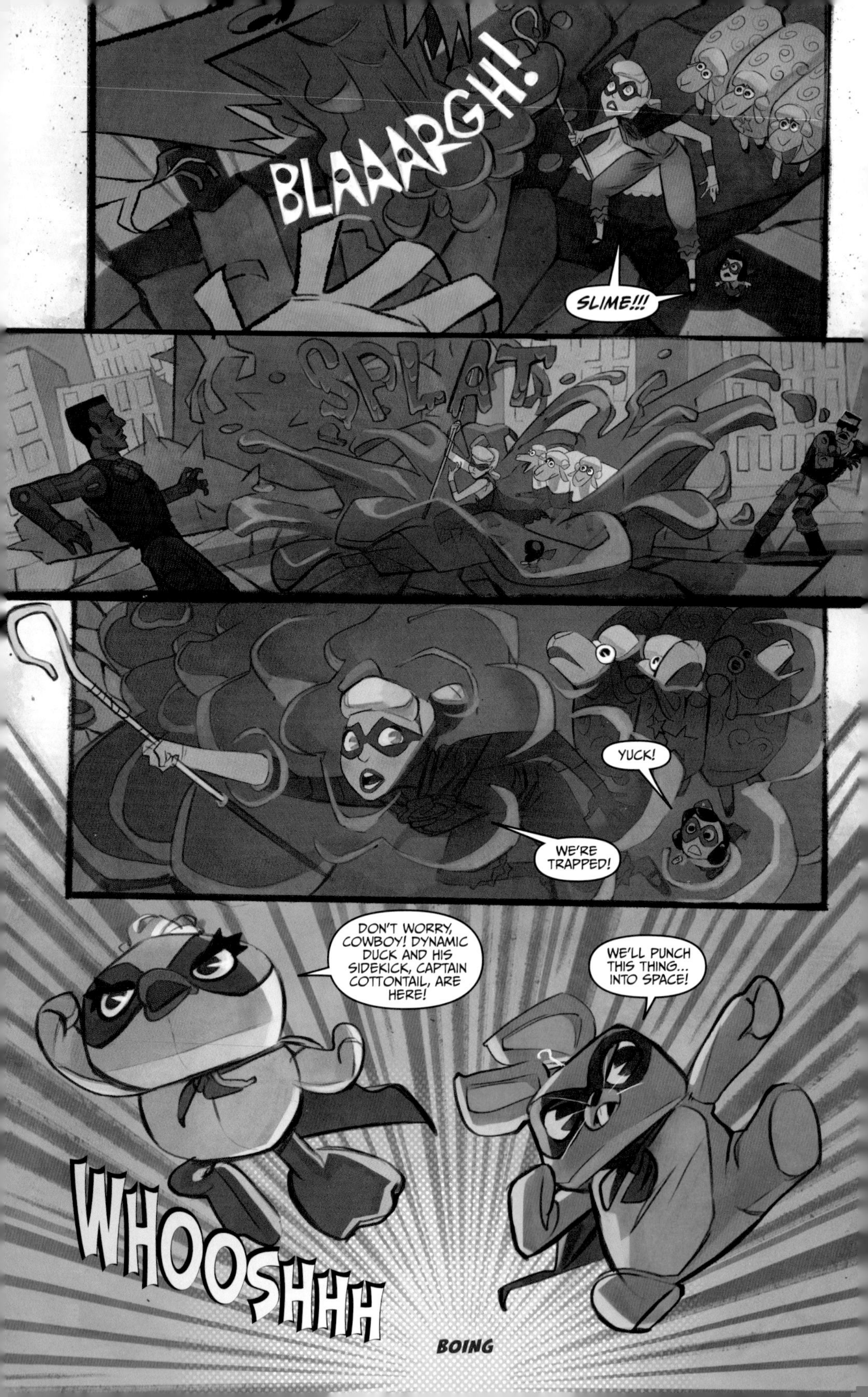
BLAAARGH!
SLIME!!!
SPLAT
YUCK!
WE'RE TRAPPED!
DON'T WORRY, COWBOY! DYNAMIC DUCK AND HIS SIDEKICK, CAPTAIN COTTONTAIL, ARE HERE!
WE'LL PUNCH THIS THING... INTO SPACE!
WHOOSHHH
BOING

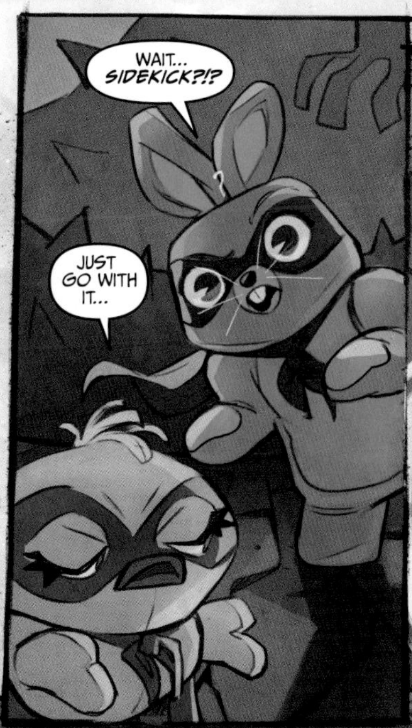
WAIT... SIDEKICK?!?
JUST GO WITH IT...
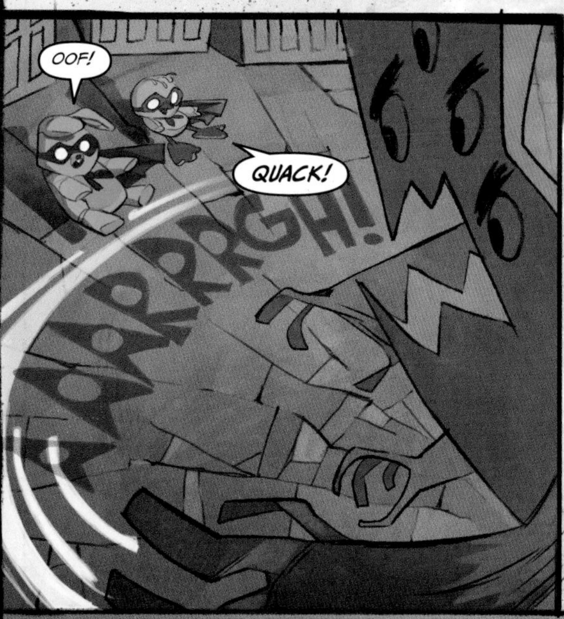
OOF!
QUACK!
AARRRGH!
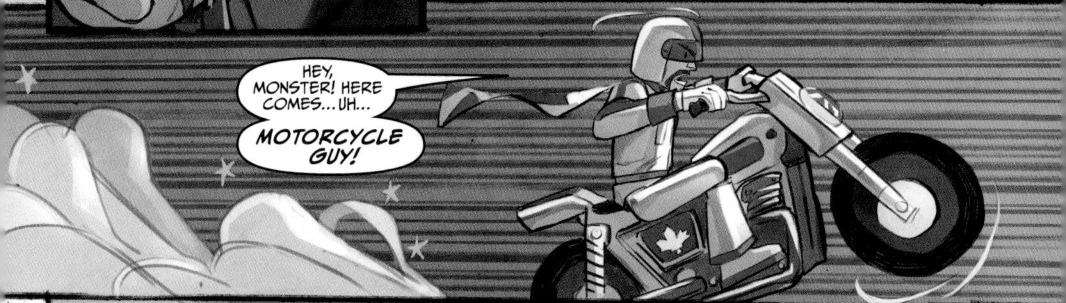
HEY, MONSTER! HERE COMES... UH...
MOTORCYCLE GUY!
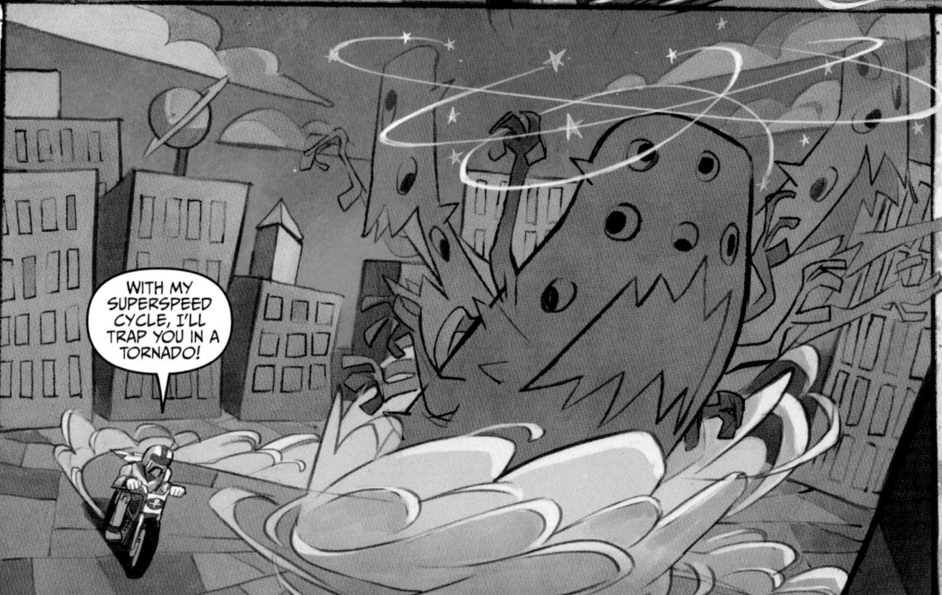
WITH MY SUPERSPEED CYCLE, I'LL TRAP YOU IN A TORNADO!

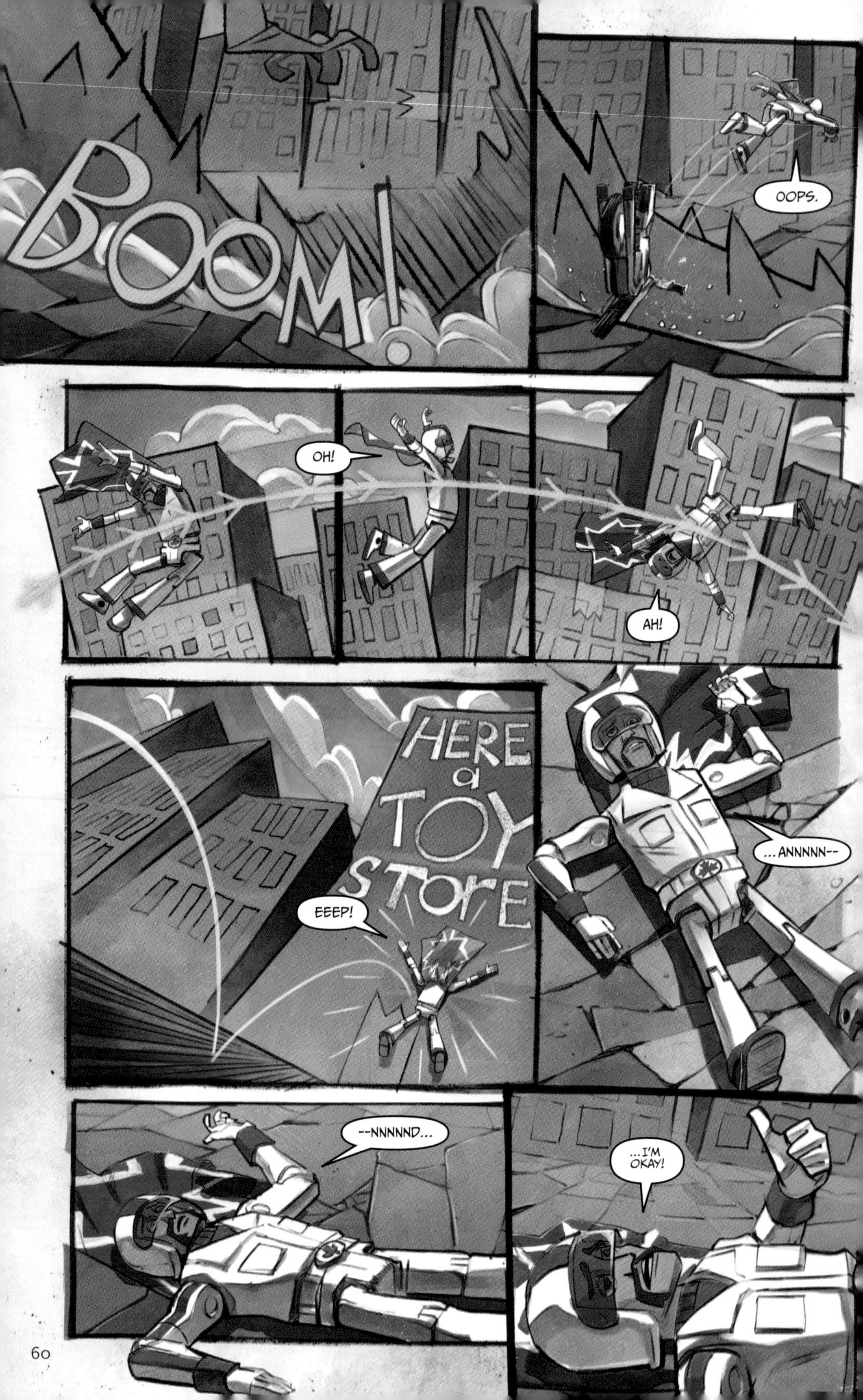
BOOM!
OOPS.
OH!
AH!
HERE a TOY STORE
EEEP!
...ANNNNN--
--NNNNND...
...I'M OKAY!

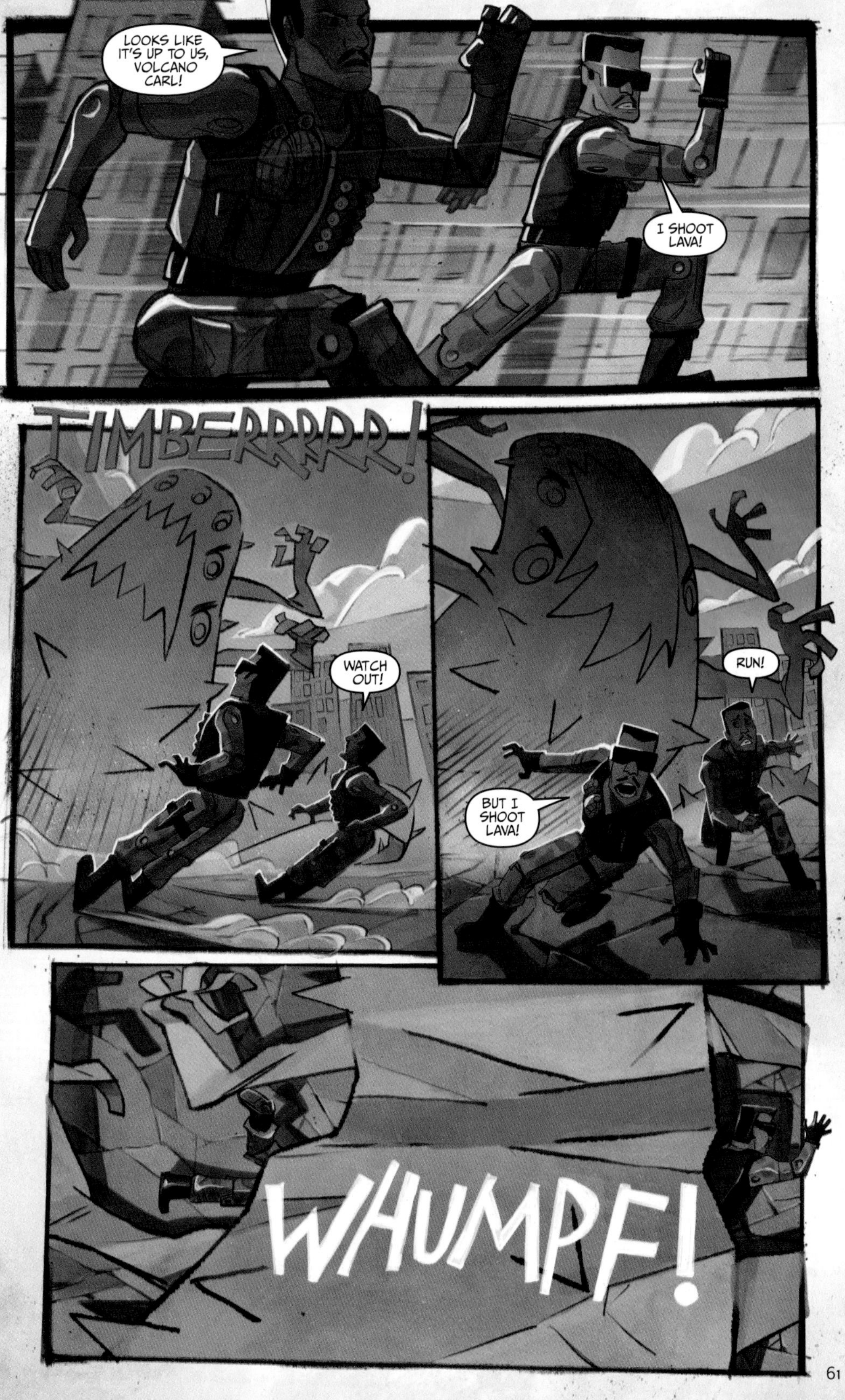
LOOKS LIKE IT'S UP TO US, VOLCANO CARL!
I SHOOT LAVA!
TIMBERRRRR!
WATCH OUT!
RUN!
BUT I SHOOT LAVA!
WHUMPF!

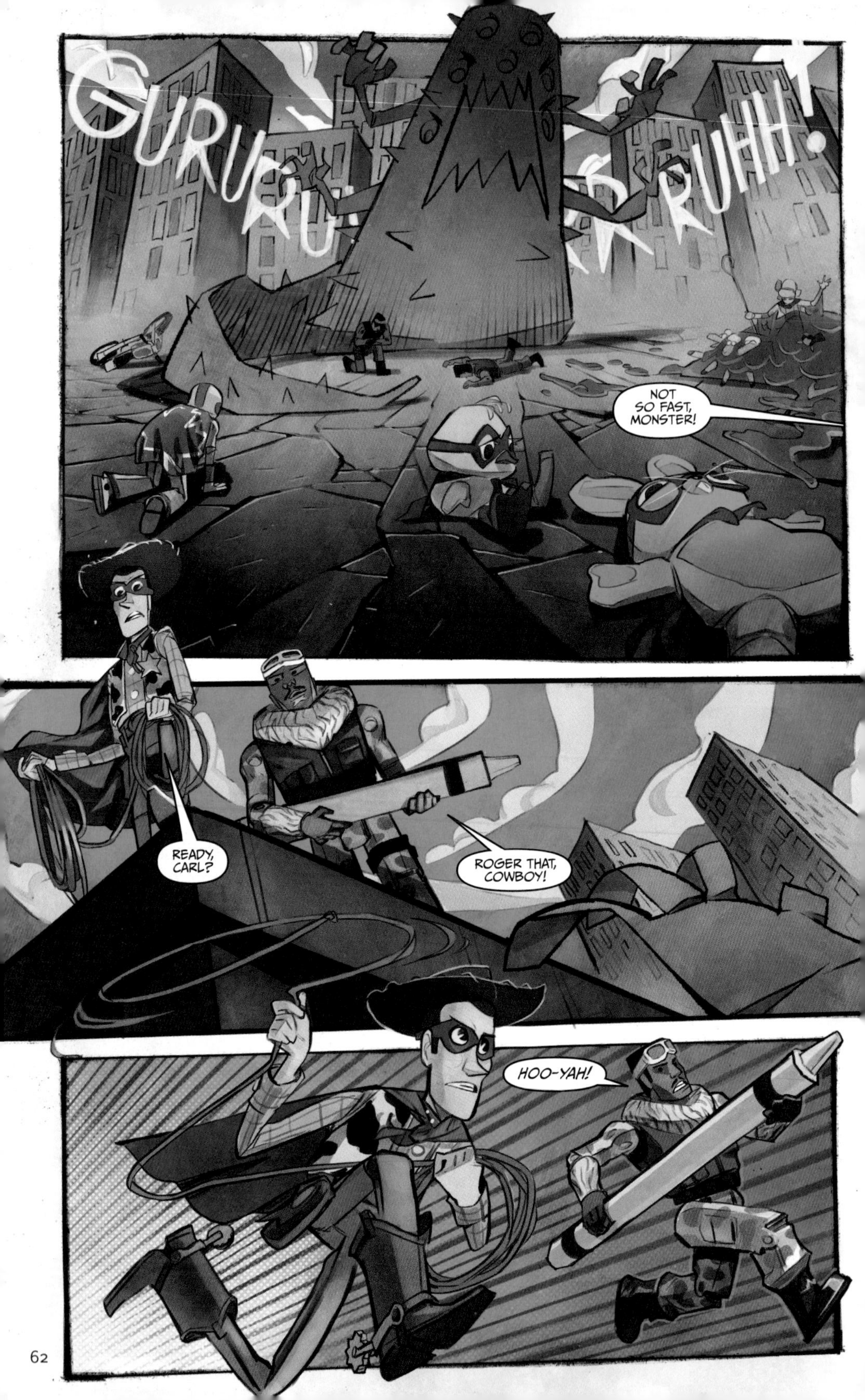
GURURUURRRUHH!
NOT SO FAST, MONSTER!
READY, CARL?
ROGER THAT, COWBOY!
HOO-YAH!

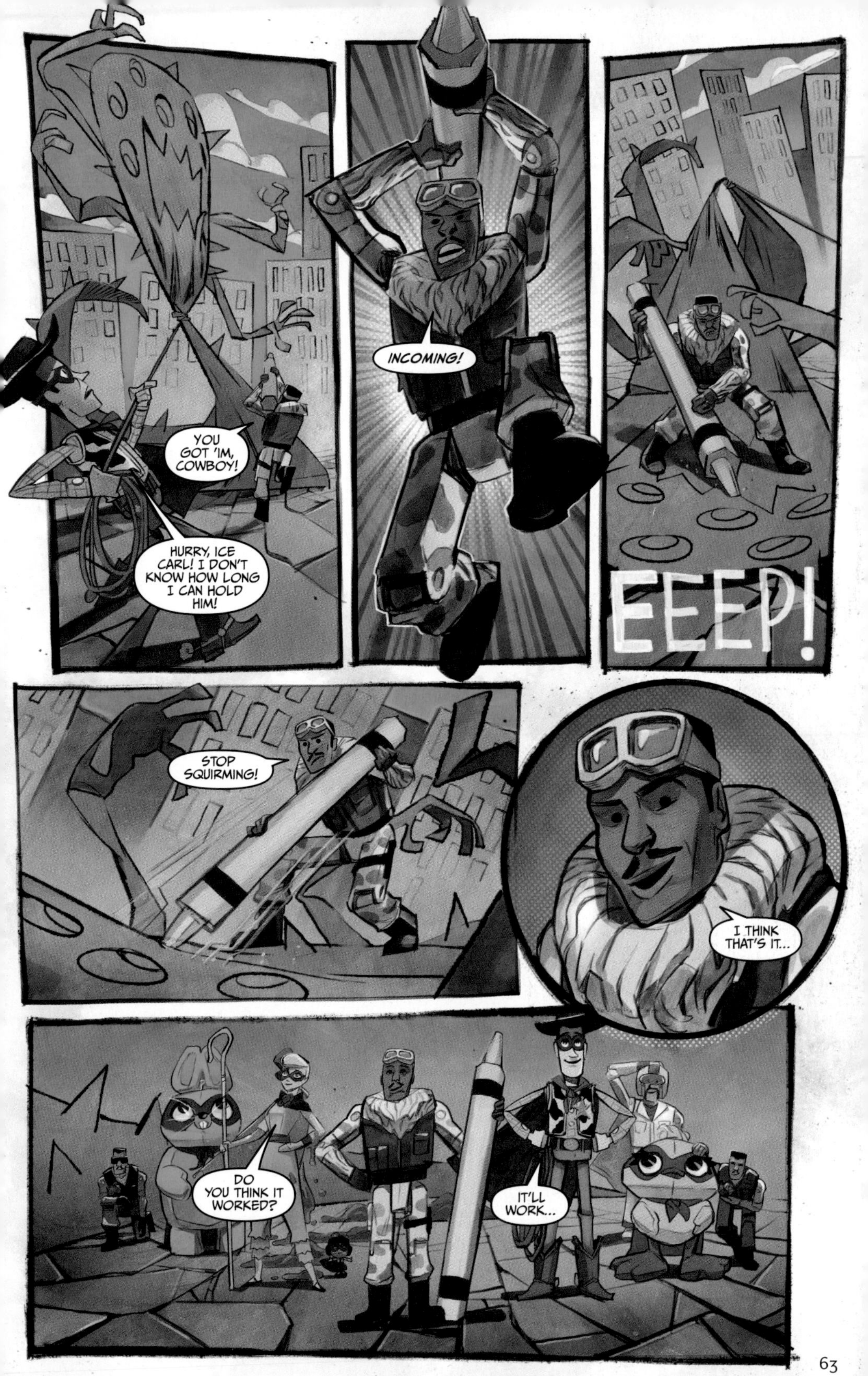
YOU GOT 'IM, COWBOY!
HURRY, ICE CARL! I DON'T KNOW HOW LONG I CAN HOLD HIM!
INCOMING!
EEEP!
STOP SQUIRMING!
I THINK THAT'S IT...
DO YOU THINK IT WORKED?
IT'LL WORK...

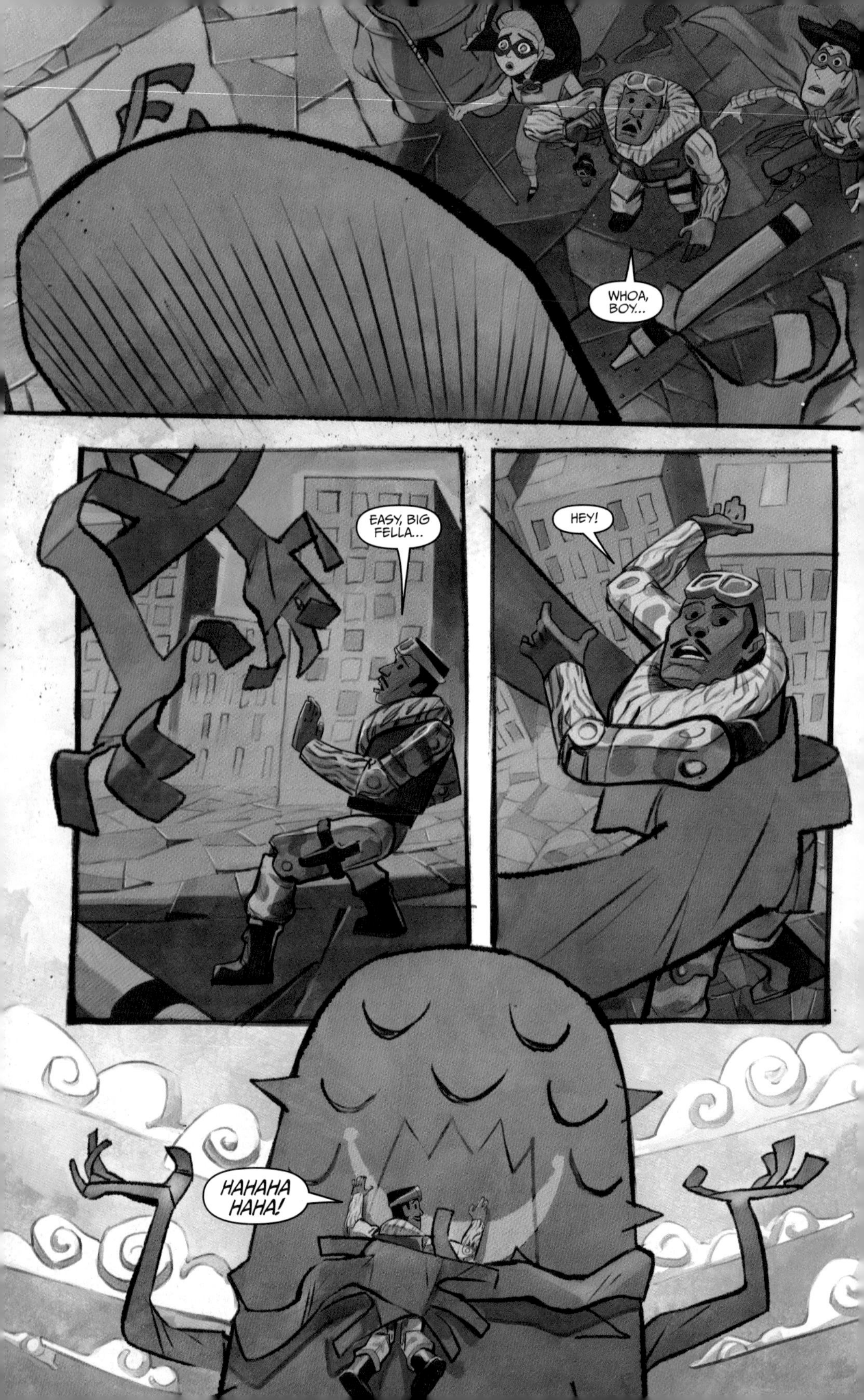
WHOA, BOY...
EASY, BIG FELLA...
HEY!
HAHAHA HAHA!

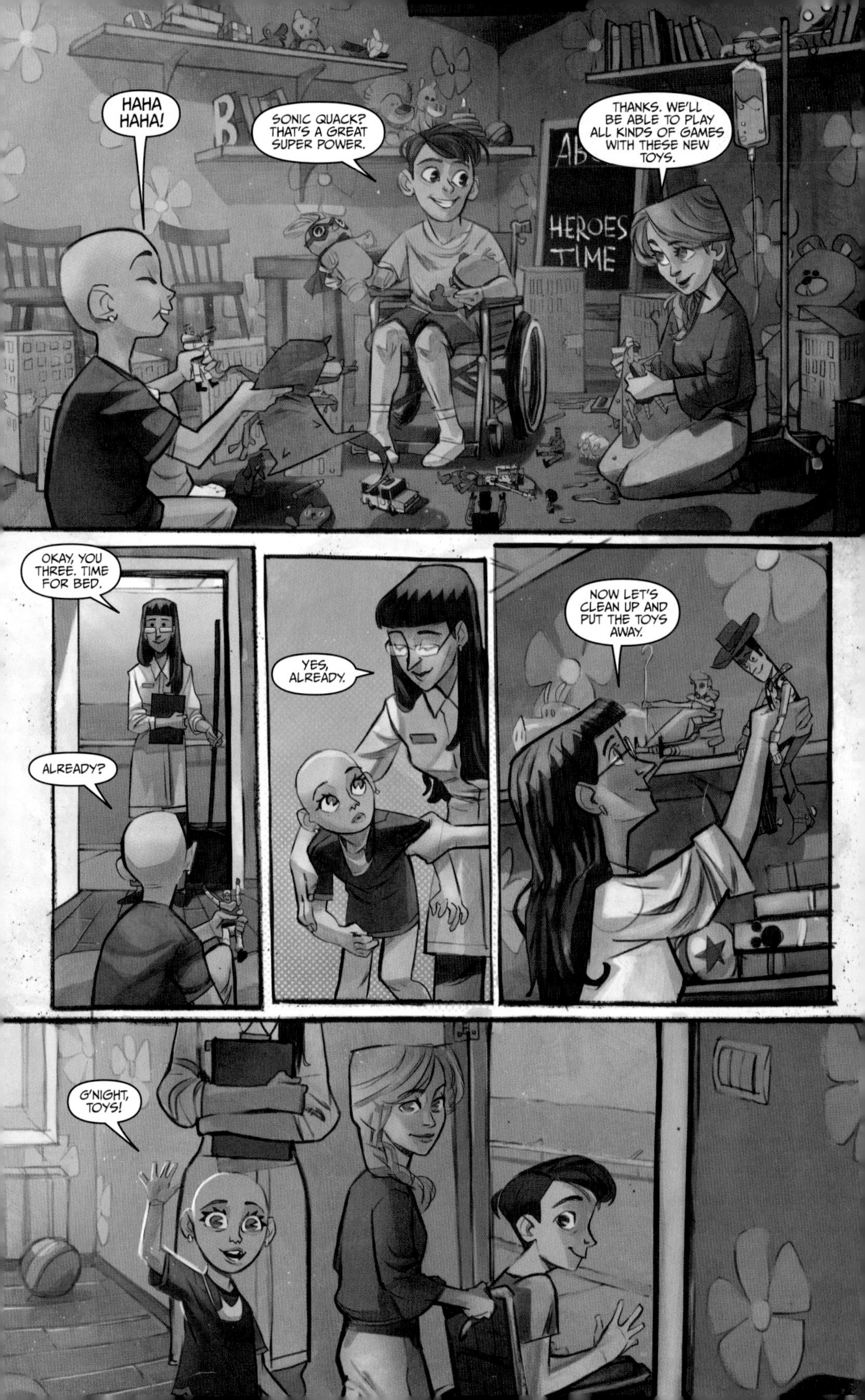
HAHA HAHA!
SONIC QUACK? THAT'S A GREAT SUPER POWER.
THANKS. WE'LL BE ABLE TO PLAY ALL KINDS OF GAMES WITH THESE NEW TOYS.
HEROES TIME
OKAY, YOU THREE. TIME FOR BED.
ALREADY?
YES, ALREADY.
NOW LET'S CLEAN UP AND PUT THE TOYS AWAY.
G'NIGHT, TOYS!

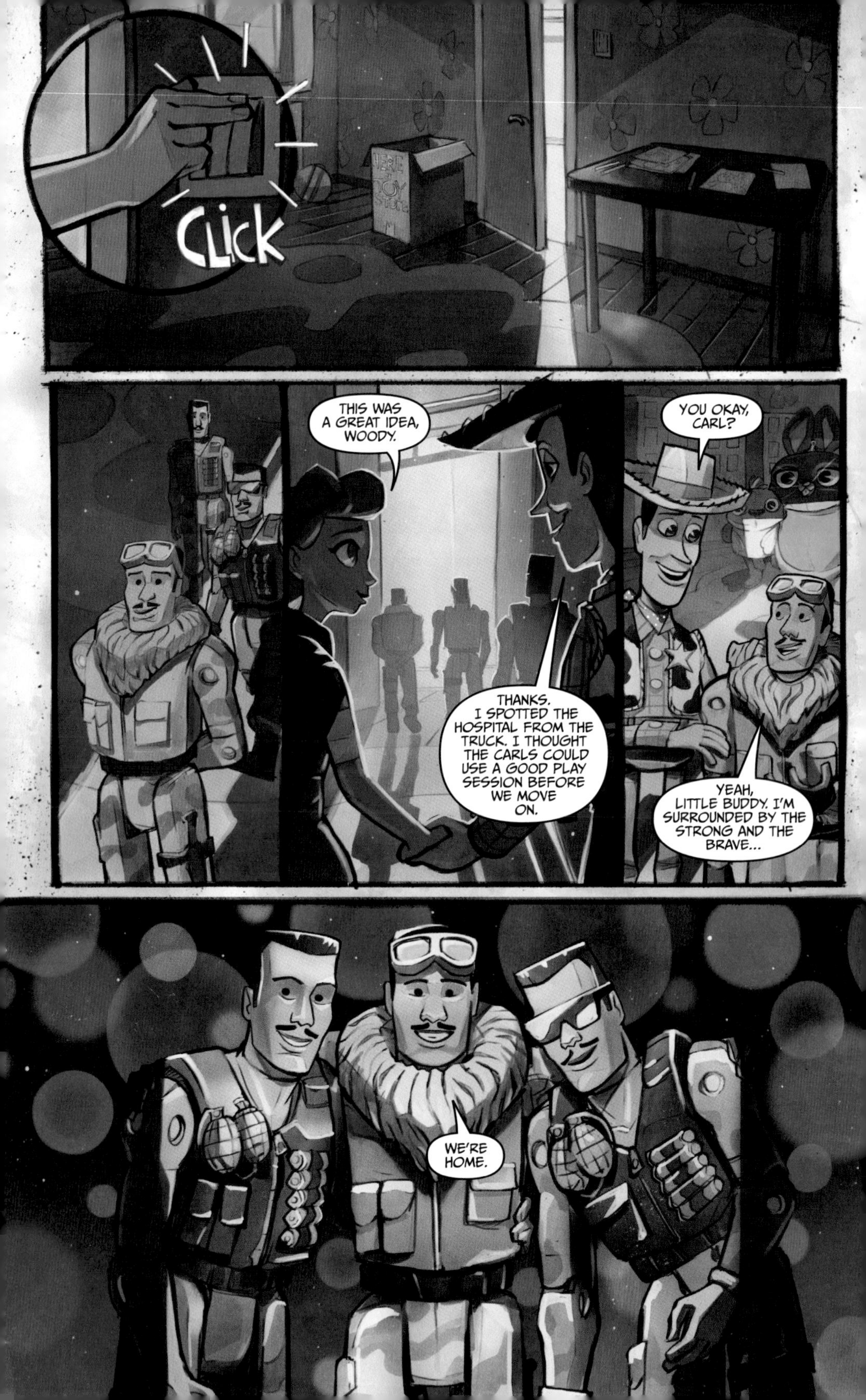

CLICK
HERE TOY STORE
THIS WAS A GREAT IDEA, WOODY.
THANKS. I SPOTTED THE HOSPITAL FROM THE TRUCK. I THOUGHT THE CARLS COULD USE A GOOD PLAY SESSION BEFORE WE MOVE ON.
YOU OKAY, CARL?
YEAH, LITTLE BUDDY. I'M SURROUNDED BY THE STRONG AND THE BRAVE...
WE'RE HOME.

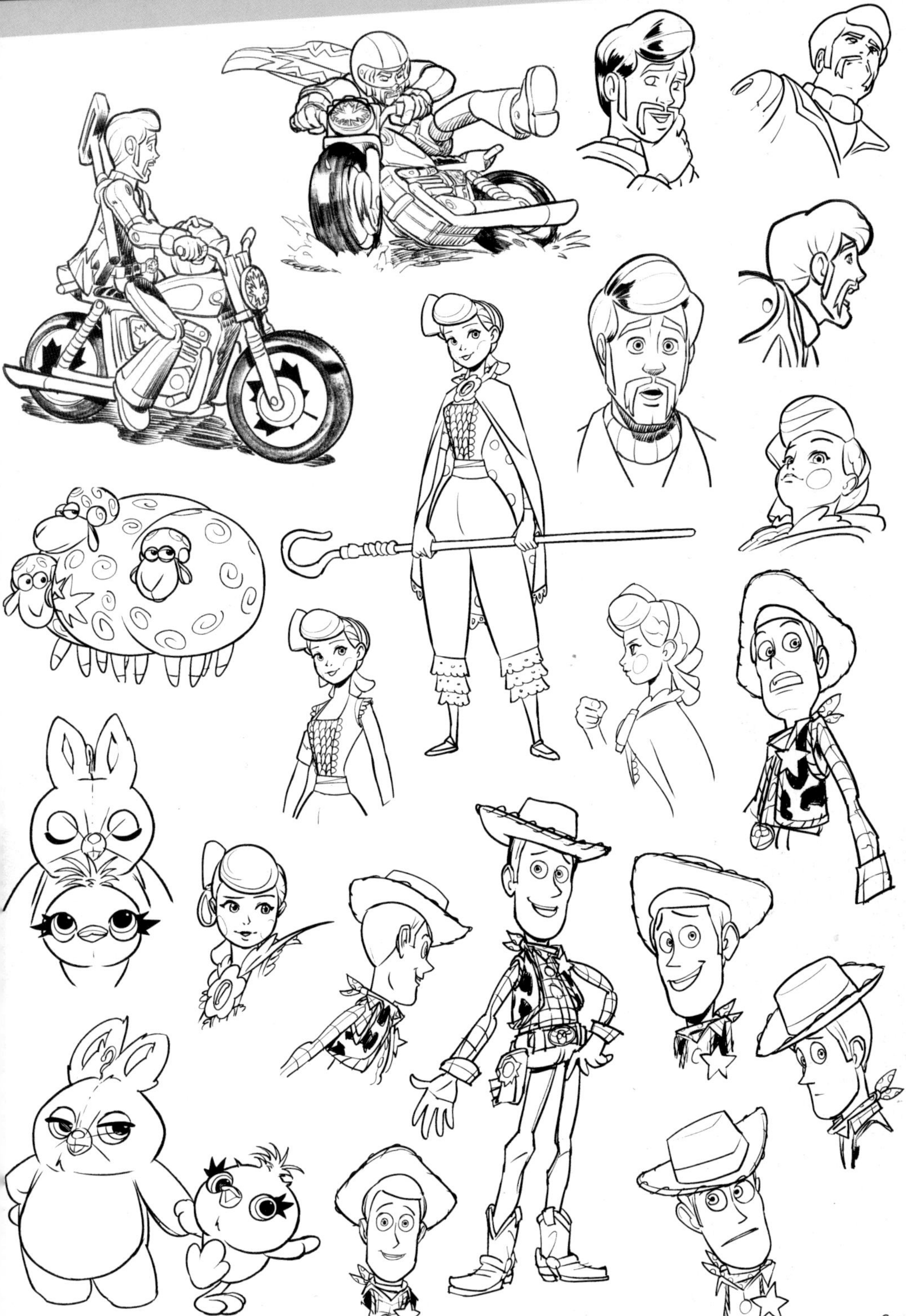

CHARACTER DESIGNS by Veronica Di Lorenzo

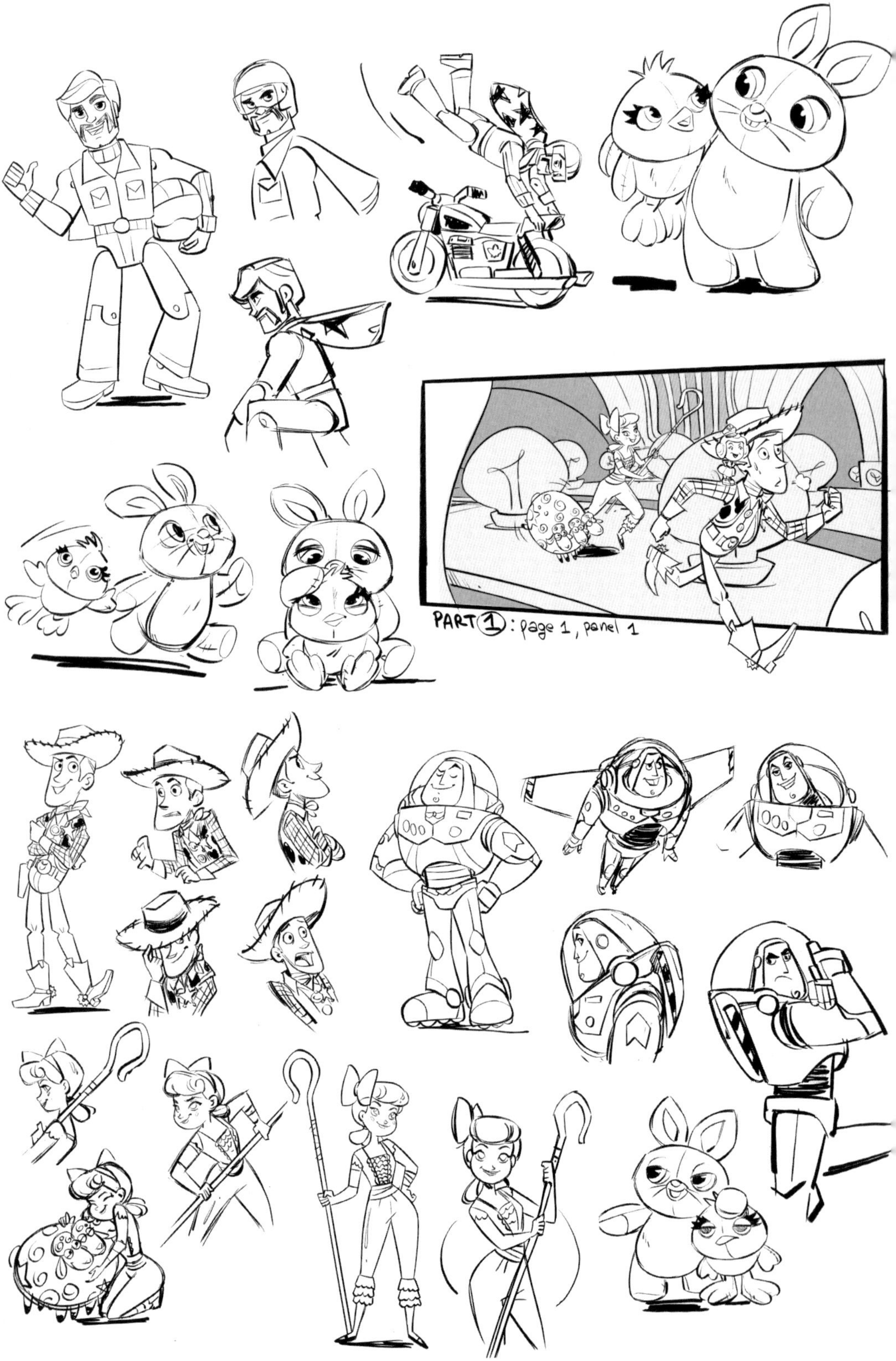
PART 1 : page 1, panel 1

TEST PANEL by Ivan Shavrin

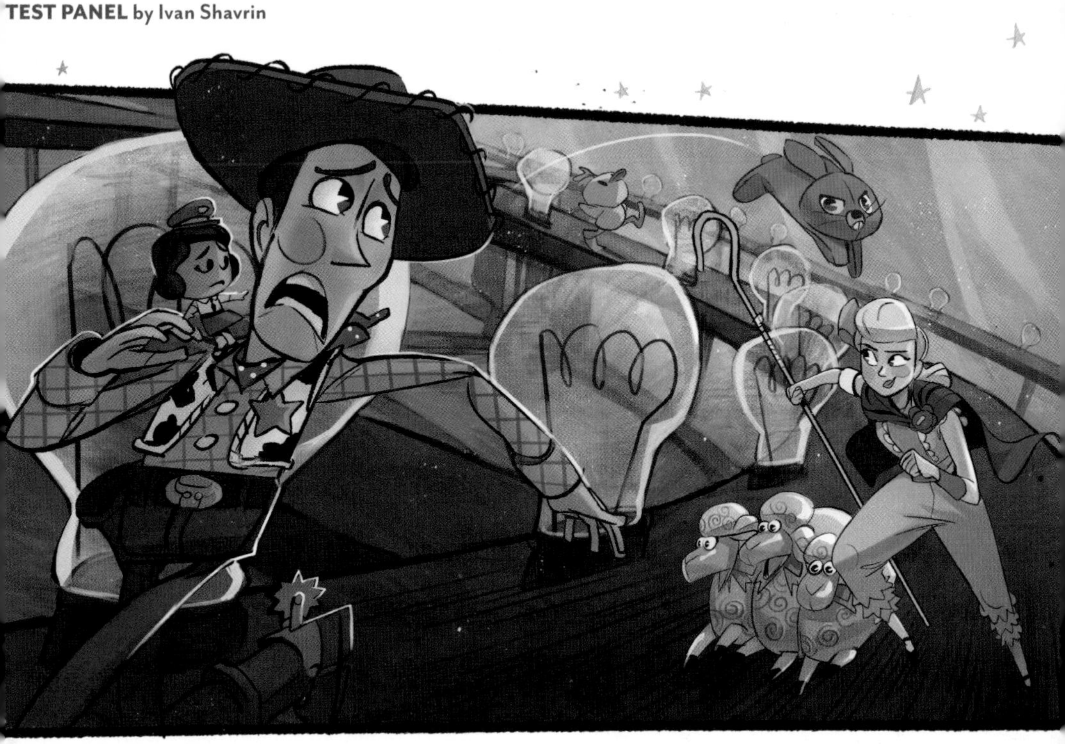

CHARACTER DESIGNS by Rosa La Barbera

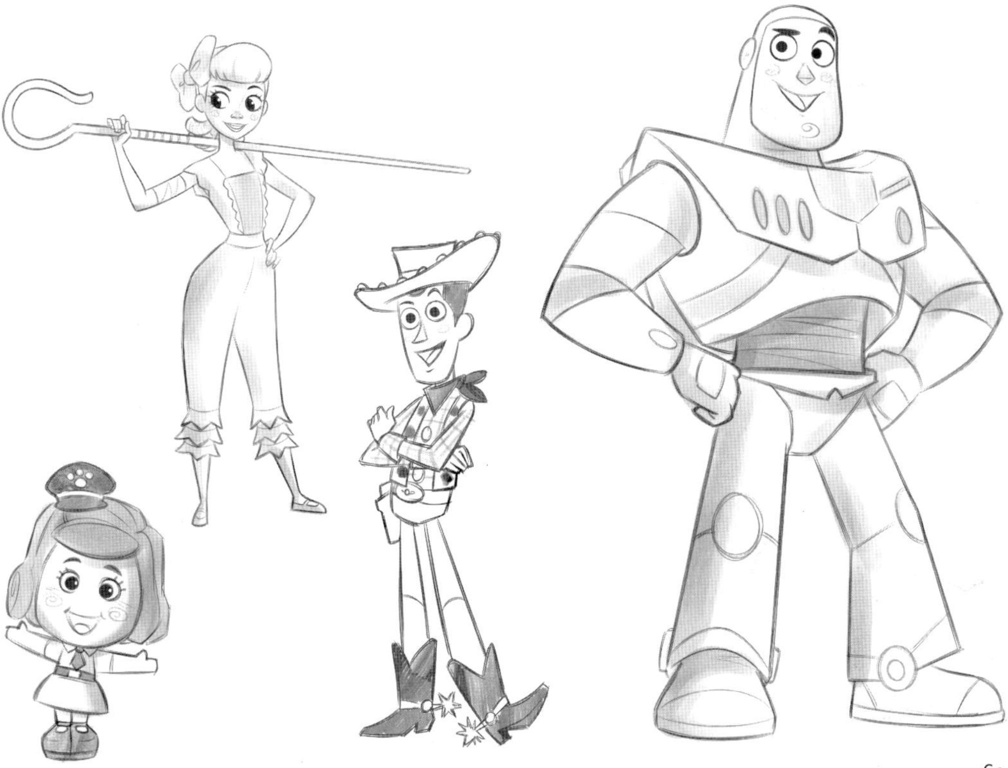

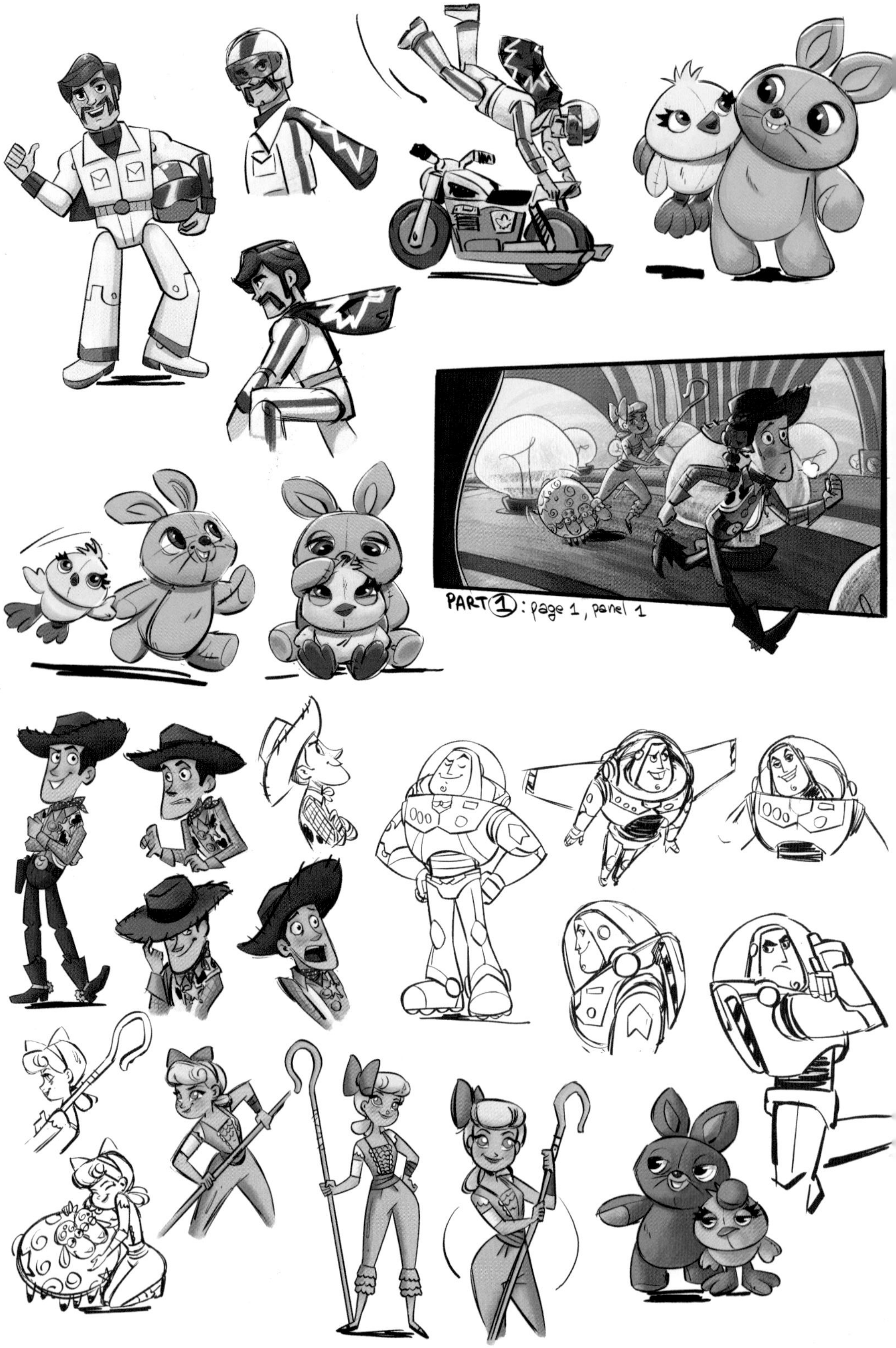
PART ①: page 1, panel 1

Disney

CLASSIC STORIES RETOLD
WITH THE MAGIC OF DISNEY!

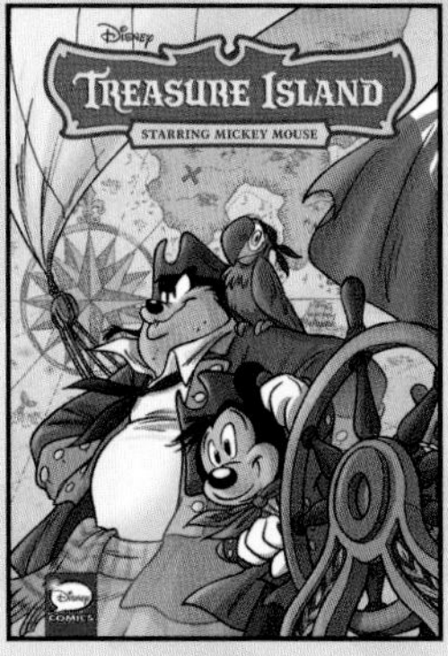
Disney
TREASURE ISLAND
STARRING MICKEY MOUSE

Disney Treasure Island, starring Mickey Mouse

Robert Louis Stevenson's classic tale of pirates, treasure, and swashbuckling adventure comes to life in this adaptation!

978-1-50671-158-4 ✠ $10.99

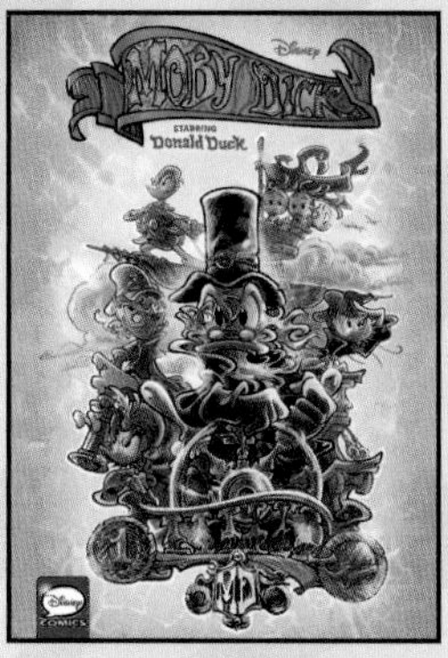
Disney
MOBY DICK
STARRING
Donald Duck

Disney Moby Dick, starring Donald Duck

In an adaptation of Herman Melville's classic, sailors venture out on the high seas in pursuit of the white whale Moby Dick.

978-1-50671-157-7 ✠ $10.99

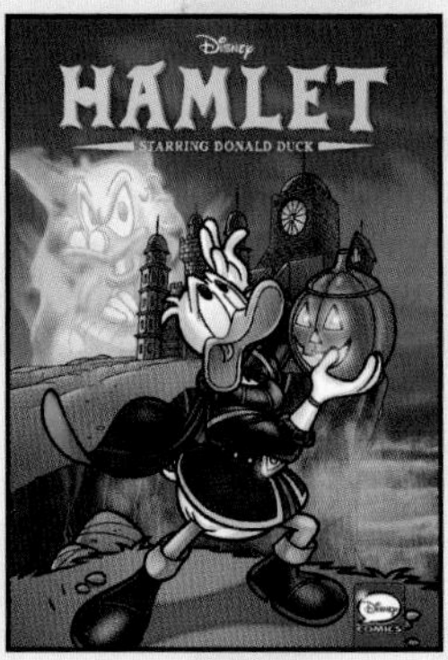
Disney
HAMLET
STARRING DONALD DUCK

Disney Hamlet, starring Donald Duck

The ghost of a betrayed king appoints Prince Ducklet to restore peace to his kingdom in this adaptation of William Shakespeare's tragedy.

978-1-50671-219-2 ✠ $10.99

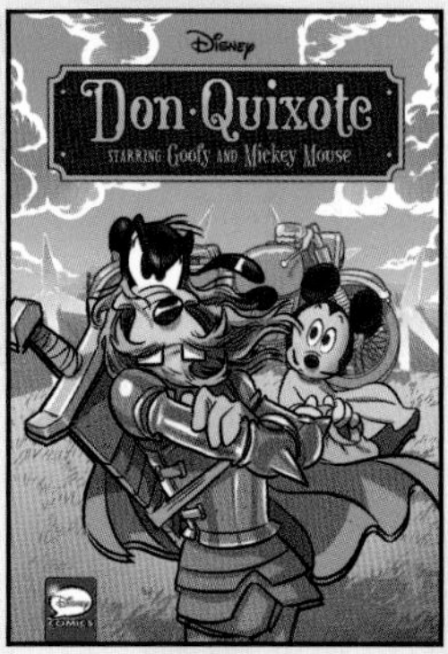
Disney
Don·Quixote
STARRING Goofy AND Mickey Mouse

Disney Don Quixote, starring Goofy & Mickey Mouse

A knight-errant and the power of his imagination finds reality in this adaptation of the classic by Miguel de Cervantes!

978-1-50671-216-1 ✠ $10.99

AVAILABLE AT YOUR LOCAL COMICS SHOP OR BOOKSTORE! To find a comics shop in your area, visit comicshoplocator.com. For more information or to order direct: ✠ On the web: DarkHorse.com ✠ Email: mailorder@darkhorse.com ✠ Phone: 1-800-862-0052 Mon.–Fri. 9 a.m. to 5 p.m. Pacific Time

DARK HORSE BOOKS

DISNEY COMICS

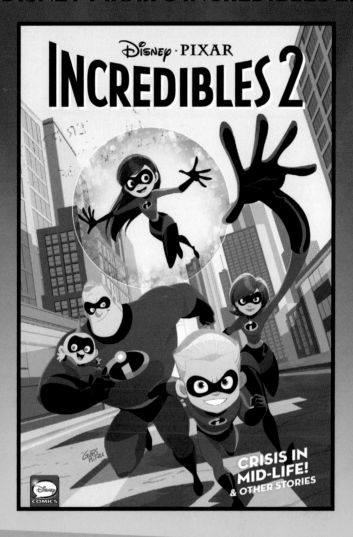